PRAISE FOR MIA HOPKINS
AND HER BOOKS

"Mia Hopkins knows how to put characters on a page."
—*Heroes and Heartbreakers*

"Beautifully descriptive...hot, sexy and full of yearning!"
—Delilah Devlin, bestselling author

"Mia Hopkins is an imaginative author who doesn't take the easy road to a formulaic book."
—*USA TODAY*

"Off the charts hot."
—*The Romance Studio*

"And those sex scenes...Holy hotness!"
—*Crystal Blogs Books*

"Sweet and filthy at the same time, just the way I like it. This book made me so happy."
—*Read All the Romance*

"I absolutely adored every inch of this book."
—*The Romance Reviews, Top Pick*

COWBOY VALENTINE

A COWBOY COCKTAIL BOOK

Mia Hopkins

Little Stone Press
LOS ANGELES

Edited by Jennifer Haymore
Cover by Syneca

Cowboy Valentine/ Mia Hopkins. -- 1st ed.
ISBN-10:
0-9979922-7-1
ISBN-13:
978-0-9979922-7-4

To Jennifer Haymore, for taking a chance on my first book and making it shine.

To Samanthe Beck, a better mentor than Yoda (and way sexier).

To Ruth Vincent-Schechtman. Thank you for your kindness, intelligence and candor in helping me bring this story to life.

To my husband, Brent, for crossing oceans, braving dark forests and killing many large insects for me over the years. I love you.

And most of all...to every "good girl" out there with a wild, rebellious heart. Keep 'em guessing, honey. This one's for you.

CHAPTER ONE

Cherry

Life will not break your heart. It will crush it.

—HENRY ROLLINS

At half past midnight, Cora decided to start closing down the shop. She shut down the soda machine by unscrewing all the sticky knobs and throwing them into the dishwasher with the last of the spoons and saucers. She stacked the clean glass dishes up on the shelves while the remaining patrons—mostly pimply teenagers on Valentine's Day dates—sucked up the last of their ice-cream sodas and fed each other final bites from banana splits.

As she filled the mop bucket in the back room, she heard the jingling of the door as a couple of patrons left the shop. Cora guessed their next stop would be the levy for some sweaty coupling in borrowed cars. Either that or chaste kisses on front porches under the eyes of shotgun-wielding fathers. Beyond that, there was not much to do in this little town. Besides beer parties out in the desert, the Oleander Ice Cream Parlor was the only place to hang out if you were underage. The two cowboy bars in town wouldn't serve minors.

Cora rarely worked at the ice-cream parlor by herself. Usually there were one or two other girls with her. But tonight they were all out on dates, so she'd worked the last four hours of the shift alone. Her last coworker had left at eight.

"You sure you're going to be all right?" Wanda had done a quick presto change-o in the washroom and had emerged in a tight green dress, her tits high and snug in their push-up bra. Wanda was twenty, a single mom of two boys aged four and three. She didn't get to go on dates very often; this was her first in months.

Cora wasn't about to ruin the evening for her. "Go on," she said, waving her hand. "I'll be all right."

"I swear, Cora." Wanda paused to apply her lip gloss. "I know you're leaving town for college soon, but you need to get yourself laid, honey. You are too pretty by far to be alone tonight."

"Boyfriend's the last thing I need." Cora served a double dip.

"I suppose you'll find yourself a nice college boy back East once you get out of Oleander." Wanda grinned. "But lemme tell you, sweetie, ain't nothing like riding a cowboy all night long."

Cora smiled and shook her head, then turned to serve a couple of wide-eyed, underaged patrons who were giggling at Wanda's cowboy comment. "You are too much, woman."

After the last kids left at five minutes to one, Cora turned off the neon *OPEN* sign in the window and stepped out to have a cigarette. Her yellow waitress uniform was thin, worn cotton, but the February night was unseasonably warm, with a dry wind whipping over the fields and blowing alternating smells of cow shit and sagebrush into town.

She sat down on a cracked concrete parking block and brushed the hair out of her face. The street was deserted. She lit up, and the flare of her cigarette seemed to be the only light in the whole town. She imagined every single person in town but her having sex, all five thousand, nine hundred and ninety-nine of them: three thousand dicks sheathed in two thousand nine hundred ninety-nine pussies or assholes or mouths. The math meant one talented lady was entertaining two men tonight.

Cora snorted at the thought. Thinking about the mechanics of sex grossed her out enough to help push down the sneaking sense of loneliness and longing that she felt rising in her chest. She'd gotten a scholarship for Brown, a big boon for a Mexican-American kid from the middle of nowhere. But studying like a maniac and working like a dog had left her little time for love, or whatever substituted for love when you were eighteen and had no idea where your life was really leading you.

The cigarette calmed her down some, so she turned back to the shop to finish closing. When she reached for the handle of the door, a pair of headlights lit up the storefront and a big engine shuddered into Park behind her.

She stubbed out her cigarette on the rim of a trash can and turned around. The driver's side door squeaked open and shut.

"We're closed," she said to the figure who walked up to her, a tall man in jeans, a plaid shirt and a cowboy hat.

He looked up in the faint light coming from the store window. "That so?" he drawled. His voice was deep.

"Afraid so." Cora squinted at him. "Do I know you?"

The man stepped farther into the light. "Maybe."

He was about six feet or so, with high cheekbones and a clean-shaven chin. His skin was tanned and freckled, as though he spent long hours in the sun. He tipped his hat back, and at once Cora saw his eyes—green but with pupils rimmed in gold. He was handsome as hell.

"You're a MacKinnon kid," she said, although she knew full well which one he was, and that he was no kid.

"Caleb."

"I remember you from school. You graduated like three, four years ago."

He looked down at her. His scrutiny scorched her cheeks. "I want to say I remember who you are, but I can't," he said at last. "What's your name?"

"Cora. Corazón Gomez."

Caleb put a boot on the parking block and hooked his thumbs onto his belt. "Wait. I think I remember you too. You were that really smart one. The freshman in my chemistry class who knew all the answers. I think I had you in Spanish too. The teacher always made a big deal about your name meaning... What was it?"

"Heart. *Corazón* means heart."

His eyes locked on hers and he nodded slowly, in no hurry to respond. To keep from fidgeting, she put her hands in the pockets of her uniform, wondering if he was going to say anything more. In the quiet, the wind rustled through the ocean of sagebrush that grew across the road.

"Well, I have to finish closing up." She tried to sound casual. "Nice seeing you again, I guess."

He still hadn't stopped staring at her, but when she broke eye contact with him and turned toward the door, he cleared his throat. "Um, any chance I could get a sundae? I've had a hell of a night. I'd appreciate it."

"I don't think I'm supposed to let you in after closing time."

"I won't tell anyone. I promise."

Cora's hand rested on the door handle for a moment. When she looked at him again, he smiled, and a deep dimple formed in his left cheek, temporarily distracting her enough to make her say, "Okay. But you have to make it fast."

"My three brothers taught me to eat quickly or not at all."

He followed her in, then sat down at the counter, took off his hat and ran his hand through his dark blond hair, disheveling it and making himself even more attractive.

Trying not to make eye contact with him, she grabbed a glass dish off the shelf and picked up the scoop.

"What'll it be?"

"Surprise me."

She fixed him a black-and-white sundae and tried not to blush under the heat of his stare as she moved behind the counter. When she spooned the bright-red cherry on top, he murmured, "Beautiful."

She put the dish in front of him. He grabbed the spoon at once and took a big bite. "That's good," he said, his mouth full.

"Can I ask you a question?" she asked, pulling out the fudge pumper. "Why are you here at the ice-cream parlor? Why aren't you at Frank's or the Silver Spur like everyone else who struck out tonight?"

"How do you know I struck out?"

"You said you'd had a rough night. I made an assumption."

He smiled. "Smart girl. I did indeed strike out. But I don't feel up to either of those bars. I know too many people there." He wiped his mouth with a napkin and took another bite. "I'd rather be here. With you."

She snorted, uncomfortable with his flirting. "No one would rather be here. *I* wouldn't rather be here with me."

"So your valentine's waiting for you at home?"

She covered up the nuts and refilled the marshmallow dispenser. "Sure. If by my valentine you mean my grandma. She drinks a glass of wine and goes to bed at eight."

"No boyfriend, Cora? I find that hard to believe." He licked a drop of whipped cream off the corner of his mouth.

She kept her eyes glued to her dishrag. "There's no point. I'm leaving in a few months."

"Where to?"

"School. Rhode Island." She walked over to him and saw that he was half-finished. He *did* eat fast. "I need to close the register. That sundae's three fifty."

He pulled out his wallet and took out a fiver. "Keep the change." He winked.

"Thanks." She rolled her eyes.

After she closed the register, she went to wipe down and sweep the tiny dining area.

When he was finished, he got up and, to her surprise, took his dish to the sink in the back room. Then he came back out with the mop.

"What are you doing?" she asked.

"Helping you out." He began to swab the sticky tile floor, leaving it shining and clean. "Seems like a raw deal to be here on Valentine's Day. At least you'll get out of here sooner than if I help."

Surprised, but not one to argue about extra help, she refilled all the napkin dispensers, then straightened up the candy counter.

"Who was she?" she asked after a while, feeling shaky and overbold at the same time.

"Who?" asked Caleb, rinsing out the mop.

"Your date."

"Oh." He hung the mop up and wiped his hands on his jeans. "A mistake is what she was."

He straightened all the chairs and then sat back down at the counter, facing her. "I've been working down at the Hughes place. She's the foreman's daughter. I finally got the courage to ask her out. I'm not sure if her old man had anything to do with it, but she stood me up. I waited for a couple of hours and then just gave up. And here I am."

"She pretty?" Cora asked, her heart pounding like a jackhammer.

He shrugged. "To be honest, she's nowhere near as pretty as you." He leaned his elbows back on the counter, his posture lazy, like that of a wolf that hasn't decided if it's going to start chasing something. "Can I ask you a question?"

She turned off the light in the back room and started to put on her jacket. "What?"

"Do you wanna go for a ride with me?"

"Where?"

He shrugged again, his mouth a line of perfect insouciance. "Anywhere. Back roads. I do it all the time."

She said nothing for a little while, but he held her fast with his eyes just the same.

"If you're planning on compromising my honor," she said, trying to make a joke even though her body felt like horses at the starting gates, "my grandma will come after you with her machete."

"I'll only compromise your honor if you want me to. Come on."

Caleb stopped at the Liquor Shack before getting on the highway. In the dark, the crescent moon rained down faint silver light and the dark hills in the distance were silhouetted against deep purple. The highway was empty.

"What did you buy?" she asked, looking at the paper sack he'd stashed by her feet.

"Beer, water, some other stuff. Are you thirsty? Help yourself."

There were some peach-flavored wine coolers in the bag, which she assumed he'd gotten for her. Since she started working at the ice-cream parlor, her sweet tooth had gone completely dead. She popped open one of his Bud Lights and took a tentative sip. It tasted like sourdough bread, not unpleasant.

"Here it is." He turned off the highway.

They bumped along a wide dirt road, and Cora closed her window against the dust rising off the tires. "Where are we?"

"On Hughes land," he said.

"Will we get in trouble for being here?"

"They've got fifteen thousand acres. They don't use this pasture until summer."

"Are you one of their cowboys?"

"Nope. I'm a ranch hand. I do the shit work no one else wants to do."

"Like what?"

"Mend fences. Muck out stables. They let me help with the branding once. I look after most of the equipment too, and fix it when it breaks."

There was a key chain hanging from the ignition, a bottle opener that said *Las Vegas* on it. It banged against his steering column as the truck swayed back and forth over the dirt road.

"You left town after graduation," she said. She remembered when he did. Her fifteen-year-old heart had split clean in two.

"I went to work ranches in Nevada first, then Montana. Same stuff I do here."

"Why'd you come back?"

"Mom asked me to," he said quietly. "My dad's sick."

"Oh," she said. He didn't say more, and she didn't ask.

He turned on his high beams just as the road got rougher and narrower, heading toward foothills covered with yellow grass and studded with oak trees. "I just got this truck—'87 Silverado 4x4. She's dinged up bad but she's got a badass engine, and the previous owner gave her a four-inch lift." He punched it, and they lurched forward.

Cora had finished the beer, so she tossed the can on the floor and clicked on her seat belt.

"Let's go," he said with a smile.

They roared up a steep hill, the tires spinning a little at the top. He turned the steering wheel to the left and gunned the engine just enough to get them over the edge. The truck wound through the scrubby trees until they reached a small clearing.

When he shut off the engine and killed the lights, the only sounds were crickets and the *ding* of cooling metal. The only light came from stars and the sliver of moon hanging high in the sky.

"Pass me a beer." He took off his seat belt.

She popped one open for him. "Can I smoke in your truck?"

"Sure."

She lit up. When her eyes adjusted to the dark, she could make out the valley below them, spread out like a black blanket, with the faint outlines of fields and orchards. Downtown Oleander was a little sprinkling of orange lights in the darkness.

"Slide over," he said. "I'm cold."

Insides shaking, she unbuckled her seat belt and tucked herself under his right arm. He smelled clean and sharp, like leather and Ivory soap. His body was hard and lean and broad; his forearm hanging over her shoulder made her feel tiny.

Without saying anything, he tipped his head forward and stole a drag from her cigarette. His lips touched her fingers. He exhaled out the open window, then took a long drink of beer.

"Feels like we could be the only people in the whole damn world right now, don't it?" He took off his hat and placed it on the bench seat beside her. "Are you nervous?"

Her voice hitched in her throat. "Nervous about what?"

"Leaving for college."

She smiled, then stubbed out the cigarette in the metal ashtray. "A little bit. Mostly I just want to get out of here."

"I felt that way too," he said. "But being back is not so bad. Helps to see the place in a different light." With a featherlight touch, he stroked her cheek and the side of her neck. The pad of his finger was calloused. "You were always so smart, though. I doubt you'll be coming back. Am I right?"

"I don't know." She felt bold enough to rest her left hand on his thigh, which was rock-hard beneath the worn denim of his jeans. "I don't know a lot of things."

"What else don't you know?" he asked. She could sense him smiling like a wolf in the dark.

"Boyfriend stuff, I guess."

"What's so bad about boyfriends?"

She shrugged. "My mom had me when she was sixteen, then ran off. A lot of my friends had kids in high school. Some got married. Some didn't." She touched the seam along his jeans. "They'll be in Oleander forever. They don't have a road out. I do."

He finished off his beer and threw the can out the window. He leaned his head against hers, then pressed his lips against her temple where her hairline met bare skin.

She closed her eyes. His heat crept through their clothes and into her body, and she felt like she was hanging over some dark precipice with only a thread holding her back.

"College boys," he said. "They're no better than the boys out here. They may have money and good grades, but they're animals too. You're going to have to watch yourself."

"Watch myself how?"

"You should know what to expect." He leaned his rigid torso into her and dipped his head down to kiss the raging pulse in her neck. His lips were so hot they seemed to scorch her skin, and she leapt back, overwhelmed by him.

"I f-feel so…" she stammered, breathless, "…like I'm hot. All over."

"Normal symptom, Doctor," he said.

"Caleb."

"Yes, Cora?"

"I've never been kissed."

"Damn, seriously?" He smiled again, and in the silence she cursed his dimple and his stupid handsome face. "Get back here, then. I've wanted to kiss you since I saw you standing in front of that shop."

She froze in place and stared at him. He was the same Caleb on whom she'd nursed a raging crush, but now he was a man. "Tell me something. Do you really remember me from back in school?" she asked.

He turned toward her. His shoulders were well built. "I remember a little girl with braided hair and glasses. What I don't remember is the beautiful woman sitting in my truck telling me she's never been kissed."

She bit her lip. "What should I do?"

"First of all, do you *want* me to kiss you?" he asked quietly.

The faint moonlight illuminated the lower half of his face. She remembered his full, perfectly formed lips, but his jaw was more angular than it was when he was eighteen. "Yes," she whispered.

"Close your eyes, then."

He put his big hand on the back of her neck and held her steady. He put his other hand in the middle of her back and pulled her into his body. Her hands rested on his rock-hard shoulders and her breasts were crushed against his chest.

And then he was kissing her.

She was too agitated to feel anything at first. She tasted the faint aroma of cherry syrup on his breath. When she peeked at him, she saw that his eyes were closed tight, so she closed hers again too.

But as the kiss went on, the sensations unraveled and she was able to identify each part. She felt the sweet glide of his top lip on hers, tender and soft in contrast to the hard muscles under her hands. He pressed his bottom lip between her lips until she opened her mouth. He kept his hand on the back of her neck as he slid the tip of his tongue between her teeth. She parted her teeth a little bit wider, and he dragged his tongue against hers, back and forth, until she began to do the same to his. When she did it, a soft groan sounded in his throat, and he tightened his arms around her. She felt a tug in her lower stomach, and her pussy clenched, wrenching up and retreating into her body.

He pulled away just enough to whisper, "First time, my ass."

She touched his face with her fingertips, unsure if he was real. "Again," she said. "Do it again."

He kissed her good and deep. Hours passed. He was in no hurry. There was a watering hole not far away and as they kissed, Cora could hear the quiet symphony of frogs gathered there for the night. In the distance, a pack of coyotes caught something and yowled like a schoolyard full of children, until it was eaten and they fell completely silent once again.

He explored the inside of her mouth with his tongue. They formed a flavor together: beer and cherries, salt and skin. She licked his teeth, lingering on the wolfish incisors she'd always thought were sexy.

He kissed her neck so achingly slowly that she felt her body collapse into a swirling core of hot liquid. By the time he'd made it back to her lips, she was trembling.

"You wanna go further, Cora?" he asked, kissing the corner of her mouth.

She nodded. She was so deep in his trance that she didn't quail when he took her hand and put it on his erection.

"Feel that?" he whispered, smiling.

Eyes wide, she rubbed the palm of her hand over the hard bump behind his fly.

"Think about it, sweetheart," he murmured. "Don't rush. It's your choice."

"What would you do if I asked you to take me home right now?" she asked.

He leaned his head back and exhaled. "I might cry a little," he said. "But I'd live."

She smiled. "What was your first time like?"

"I was about your age. A woman in Montana. She brought me home from a bar. She must've been about thirty-five. She made sure her kids were asleep then took me into her bedroom."

"That doesn't sound so good."

"I didn't know any better. I was drunk as a skunk." He kissed her again, stroking her cheeks with the sides of his thumbs as she rubbed him through his jeans. "Tell you what," he said. "Let me fix up the back. I want to lie down with you."

"It's cold."

"I've got blankets."

She watched from the cab. He put the tailgate down and lined the floor of the bed with a thick pile of Mexican blankets.

"Come on out." He opened the door for her.

He helped her climb into the truck bed and they lay down together. He threw a blanket over them both and settled down beside her, nuzzling her neck and throat. The blankets smelled of clean hay and fresh air, as though he'd just pulled them down from the wash line.

"What do you want, Cora?" he asked.

"I want you to sleep with me," she whispered. "I want you to be my first."

He kissed her closed eyelids—one, then the other. "It will hurt. Probably a lot."

"I know," she said.

He stroked her bare arms under the blankets and slowly unbuttoned the front of her uniform. The buttons went all the way down to her hemline, and when he was finished, she sat up and slid off the whole dress. He took off her shoes and socks, and she leaned back on her elbows, trying to make out his expression in the darkness. He reached behind her and unhooked her bra, letting it slide forward and releasing her breasts to the cold air and his waiting hands.

"Jesus," he hissed. "Gorgeous."

He leaned her back and kissed her neck while his big hands kneaded her tits. He worked her aching nipples between his fingers, pinching them lightly as she moaned into his mouth. Then he pinched them a little bit harder, and she felt her whole body surge with what felt like a wave of fresh, hot blood.

He dipped his head and put his lips on her left nipple, suckling her gently as he rolled her right nipple between his thumb and forefinger. Her nerve endings fired like sparklers, the sensations almost too intense for her to handle.

Caleb released her nipple. It was tiny and hard as a pebble, shiny with his saliva. "You have beautiful tits, Cora."

She reached forward and undid the snap buttons of his shirt. Underneath he wore a white-cotton T-shirt that he pulled over his head, revealing a torso rigid with muscles and smooth, tanned arms that made her pussy weep with yearning. When he covered her with his body, his feverish, smooth skin seemed to brand her, and she moaned with the pleasure of it.

"Still feeling hot?" he whispered in her ear. He licked her earlobe, and she dug her fingernails into his back without meaning to. He hissed, sucking up air between his teeth.

"Holy Jesus," he murmured.

He hooked his thumbs into the waistband of her cotton panties and began to pull them off. They were soaked and clung to her sex for a moment, until he peeled them away, releasing the sweet, elemental scent of her pussy.

Before he could touch her, she said, "Yours too," and she pointed at his jeans.

He sat up, pulled off each boot and chucked it over the side of the truck.

She sat up on her knees and ran her hands over the swollen muscles of his pecs. He had tiny pink nipples that grazed her fingertips and a chest lightly covered with dark hair. He had a shallow six-pack and deep lines along his hips that showed at the tops of his jeans.

She reached forward and undid the buttons on his fly. Smiling, he pulled another long kiss from her before he yanked his jeans off, boxers and all, and his penis sprang at her.

Cora gasped. *What the hell?*

Kneeling, he took himself in his hand and gave his cock a stroke. It stood up straighter, pointing at her like an accusation. "Never seen one before?" he asked.

In books, she thought, staring. *On Greek statues.* Not in real life, and definitely not one as big and erect as Caleb MacKinnon's.

"Touch it," he said.

"How?"

He took her hand and wrapped it around his shaft. Her fingers and thumb couldn't span his girth. His cock was dry and hot, and the skin was smoother than she thought possible. When he squeezed her hand to show her how to hold him, she felt blood pulsing just beneath the surface of his skin. He took her wrist and pushed her hand back and forth to show her how he liked to be stroked.

"Grip harder." He was breathless.

She did. His cock jerked forward, growing even more rigid in her hand. A drop of clear liquid appeared at its tip. He slid the pad of his thumb over the head. Then he held his thumb to her lips.

Without being asked, she flicked her tongue over his thumb. When he pressed it against her bottom lip, she opened her mouth and began to suck on it, her eyes never leaving his.

Slowly, he pulled his thumb from her mouth and leaned forward to kiss her. He held her against his chest as she worked his cock in her fist, and he groaned when she ran her own thumb over his glans.

"Enough," he growled, pulling her hand away. He pushed her back onto the pile of blankets. "Open your legs."

She leaned back on her elbows and did as he told her. With his big hands, he spread her knees farther apart, opening her wet pussy to the cool air. She was breathing quickly, her chest rising and falling with shallow breaths.

He ran his fingers up and down her outer labia, parting the soft hair and exposing the aching, swollen folds of her pussy lips. Cora was glad for the cover of darkness, for she had never before been naked with a man, never before even looked at herself this way.

He caressed the tender flesh with the tips of his fingers. "Do you touch yourself?" he asked.

"Sometimes," she said.

"When?"

"At night. When I can't stand it."

"Do you make yourself come?"

She swallowed as his fingers began to part her folds. "I think so," she whispered. "I'm not sure."

With a smirk, he lay down on his stomach and propped himself up on his arms. She could see the curve of his biceps in the dark and feel his warm breath on her pussy. Then he covered her with his hot mouth, kissing her long and deep where a man had never even touched her.

She pushed her head back into the blankets and felt her mind go completely blank. She felt his tongue slide into her, and if he hadn't held her legs open, she would have clamped them shut in surprise.

"Shh," he said, pulling away. He ran two of his fingers along her lips and spread them apart, opening her up even farther with a sound like a soft kiss. "You're so wet," he whispered. "And so delicious."

His hot tongue slid against her again, making her body weep with longing. He tongued her slowly until her toes uncurled and she released the arch of her back, paralyzed with arousal in the bed of his truck, her feet on the rails, her body completely immune to the cold night air.

Before she could react, he replaced his tongue with his finger and slid it into her with a tiny pinch. She whimpered and squirmed, but fell silent and still when he began to flick the tip of his tongue against her aching clitoris, strumming it back and forth until she stopped clenching at his finger. In response, he pushed his finger in deeper and began to slowly fuck her with it. Her pussy sucked wetly at him.

"I'm gonna open you up, Cora." His voice was ragged and deeper than before. "You focus on relaxing, okay, sweetheart?"

She nodded weakly and shut her eyes. Her body seemed to both crave and rebel against what he was doing to her. He ran the flat of his tongue up and down her pussy lips, then sucked her clitoris as hard as he had sucked her nipples. When she flexed her ass in response, he slipped another finger into her, and she keened with pain and pleasure.

"Shh." He rubbed her inner thigh with his other hand. "You're tiny, Cora." He shook his head. "There are other things we can do. You sure you want me to go on?"

"Yes," she said, breathless.

"I feel like I might break you."

"That's the point, isn't it?"

He growled at her words. He continued to lick her, then gently began to thrust his fingers back and forth in her tight sheath. She felt her flesh straining around him, but she gritted her teeth against the ache and focused on pulling him in instead of pushing him out. When she moaned, he flicked his tongue harder at her clitoris.

He pulled his fingers out, then tucked his hands behind her knees and pushed her legs up closer to her chest. He dipped his head down once again and began to carve his tongue through her labia. He pressed the tips of his two fingers back into her and thrust them in and out, all the while sucking on her aching clit.

After a little while, Cora opened her eyes. The sky began to lighten a little bit on the eastern horizon, and the frogs at the watering hole went quiet.

And still he continued to tongue her, keeping the same steady rhythm. She combed her fingers through his hair, then rubbed and squeezed her own breasts until her nipples were tiny pips.

His rhythm was as steady as a freight train. His fingers delved deeper into her, and after a while she felt only pleasure from them, no pain. Soon she felt the back of his ring finger stroking at her slick perineum, and the tip of his little finger pressing against her tight asshole. She gasped, and he curled his fingers inside her, hitting a sweet spot that fired spikes of pure pleasure into her brain.

"Holy shit," she rasped.

He quickened his tongue on her clit, playing the tight bud until all she saw behind her closed eyelids was white light. He began to fuck her hard with his fingers, so fast that she heard the wet smack of his knuckles against her stretched pussy lips. He curled his fingers even more, and at once she felt herself begin to lose control of her body.

"Caleb," she gasped. She opened her eyes. The last of the stars were still visible. He pushed the tip of his finger into her ass.

She came at once. Her back arched and her mouth flew open. Her screams cut through the silent darkness and echoed through the hills like the whoops of the coyotes once they got hold of their quarry. Her whole body seemed to contract around his hand, her pussy and ass thrown under wave after wave of mindless pleasure. Caleb had released with his tongue and fingers eighteen years of sexual tension, and now she was drowning in it, gasping for air.

As she rode out the last jolts of her orgasm, he began to stroke himself back to life.

"It has to be now, sweetheart," he gasped. His lips were slick with her juices.

She nodded, still in shock.

He reached into the pocket of his jeans for a condom and rolled it on quickly. The smell of rubber reached her nose, a strange note in the cocktail of smells from her body, his skin, the dry, sweet grass and the night air of Oleander.

He lay above her, a big shadow kissed by starlight. His skin was smooth and feverish. He leaned down to kiss her, hard, and she tasted her pussy juices coating his tongue.

Distracted by his lips, she suddenly felt him push the head of his cock into her. Her slick pussy lips strained around it. With the tip of his thumb, he drew tiny circles on her clitoris, and she felt the heat begin to build again.

She put her hands on his rock-hard buttocks, which he flexed as he made tiny thrusts into her, chiseling into her flesh.

She looked down and saw that his eyes were shut and his brows were drawn as if in concentration. He gave her one inch, then two.

Through the layers of pleasure he had built inside her, she felt the pain begin to surface, rushing at her. She had nowhere to go.

He was halfway inside her when he broke their kiss and looked her in the eyes. To her surprise, he looked angry, even though his words were spoken in a whisper. "Are you all right?"

She was half-impaled by his massive cock, on her back with her legs in the air, in his '87 Silverado with a four-inch lift. The night sky was licking dew all over them. She felt the weight of the world in the weight of his body, and she knew he was about to break her and brand her. She licked her lips and tightened her hold on his hips.

"Do it," she said.

At once, he straightened his legs and pushed himself forward with his feet, thrusting his cock balls deep into her virgin pussy. He groaned deep in his chest.

She made no sound except for the rush of air that escaped from her lungs as he tore into her. The pain was intense. Hot tears welled in her eyes and ran down her temples, soaking her hair.

Eyes closed tight again, Caleb supported himself on his big arms, then began to fuck her as though she weren't a virgin, as though her pussy wasn't stretched raw around his cock. He thrust back and forth, his sinuous body undulating above her, beads of perspiration bleeding into a thin sheen on his torso.

When she twisted under him with the pain, he shifted his weight and put a hand behind her knee, pinning her to the bed of his truck while he took his pleasure. The smell of hot rubber and the earthy tang of blood filled her nose and she breathed deep, trying to will the pain away.

"God gave you one tight pussy, Cora," he said, looking down at her. She was mesmerized by the lean functionality of his body. He ran his hand through his hair and rubbed the back of his forearm against the sweat on his upper lip.

"I need to come," he gasped. He grabbed the base of his cock and pulled slowly out of her.

The pain disappeared at once, replaced by a throbbing ache.

He moved back onto the tailgate. "I want to fuck you from behind. Turn around. Get on all fours."

Shaking, she crawled into position, facing away from him. Even in the darkness, she could see faint streaks of blood on the insides of her thighs and on the front of his.

Caleb grabbed her hips and dragged her backward towards him. He pushed on her upper back and she went down on her forearms, her ass thrust in the air and tipped up toward him like an offering. She felt powerless. The tears were still running down her cheeks.

He rubbed the head of his cock over her swollen pussy lips, then grunted once as he thrust back into her, all gentleness gone. He grabbed her right hip and put his opposite foot flat on the bed of the truck, his leg bent at the knee and his inner thigh pressed against the left side of her body. He began to ride her hard, all muscle and meat and urgency.

She felt the suspension of his truck bounce with the force of their fucking. In a haze, she felt her body give way to him. Something inside her seemed to rupture, and the pain, less sharp, became something different. Lust. Need.

He began to murmur endearments mixed with filth. He sounded like he was speaking in tongues. "You want this cock?" he whispered. "You want this cock in that virgin pussy? You want me to fuck your beautiful, fresh little cunt, Cora? Is that what you want, sweetheart?"

Right on the precipice of his own orgasm, he slammed into her, again and again, pulling out almost completely and sliding himself back in, the plump head of his cock kneading hard against the inner walls of her pussy. Her tits were hanging down, jiggling with each thrust. He reached forward and cupped them possessively, squeezing them and pinching at her nipples until she whimpered with both pain and arousal.

She reached back and felt the shaft of his cock sliding into her, coming out slick with her juices. She began to rub her own hard clit, and the ache began to build as he drove into her with mad hunger.

In a moment, her mind fell away, and all she became was her body, her tits in his hands, her tender cunt stretched and distended by his cock. Their bodies, slick with sweat and cold dew, crashed together in a single, powerful orgasm that crushed and shook them like prey in the jaws of a wolf.

Cora's body jerked and bucked against his, no longer under her control, pleasure and pain knifing through her nervous system and tearing it to shreds. In desperation, she reached back and held on to his hips, feeling his muscles contract as he shot long, endless spurts of come.

When it was over, he collapsed onto her back. Her arms trembled under his weight.

"Oh my God," he whispered. "Oh my God."

He fed her. Eggs and toast and coffee at a truck-stop diner thirty miles from town, where they prayed no one knew them. The windows of the diner were painted with hearts and cupids. *Ask Us about Our Valentine's Day Specials*, said a sign on their table.

Caleb was back to his gentlemanly self. He'd helped to wash off her legs by holding the water bottle while she scrubbed the blood away. The water was cold and they'd laughed about it. She didn't have a comb with her and was afraid to look at her reflection in the shiny napkin dispenser.

They sat in the booth on the same side, his arm slung lazily over her shoulder. He'd set his cowboy hat on the seat opposite them.

"When do you leave?" he asked.

"August."

He drank his coffee black. "February to August is a long time."

"Boyfriend's the last thing I need," she said automatically.

Caleb smiled. "We've got something in common, then. I ain't in the market for a boyfriend neither."

He drove her home and dropped her off at the corner so that her grandma wouldn't see his truck.

"What'll you tell her?" he asked.

"That I had to stay late and I slept in the back room."

"Will she believe you?"

Cora smirked. "Probably not."

"Hide her machete for me, then."

She got out, and he kissed her once more through the driver's side window. He'd rolled up his sleeves. There was a small tattoo on the inside of his right forearm that she hadn't seen in the dark. She reached into the truck and pulled his arm forward to look at it in the light. The ink was dark and new.

Heartbreaker.

"What time do you get off work tonight?" he asked.

Cora looked up at him. In the morning sunlight, his eyes were bottle green. There was danger in every single beautiful thing about him. "I'm leaving soon. We shouldn't see each other."

He narrowed his eyes at her. "What time?"

She sure as hell didn't want to fall in love, but the dull, unfamiliar ache between her legs began to throb like a heartbeat. As soon as she opened her mouth, she realized that she wanted to see him again. Badly. For once, she considered the possibility that the good girl and the rebel inside her sometimes spoke with the same voice. "Eight thirty."

Caleb reached forward and stroked her cheek with the back of his thumb. "See you then, sweetheart."

She could feel him watching her. As she walked up the driveway of her grandmother's tiny clapboard house, she heard Caleb start up the truck. His souped-up engine roared and shook the ground under her feet, sending sweet vibrations up her spine.

CHAPTER TWO

The Last Time

Every day I wonder how many things I am dead wrong about.

—JIM HARRISON

Merle Haggard's "Workin' Man Blues" buzzed from busted speakers as Caleb pulled up the long driveway of his family's ranch. His mother reached over his snoozing father to crank the window closed against the rising dust. Without air-conditioning, the truck cab sweltered in the summer heat.

Caleb stopped at the front porch, and his mother squeezed his father's arm, just above the faded Navy tattoo that said *Heartbreaker*. Caleb had gotten an identical tattoo one drunken night out alone after he'd found out his dad's cancer had returned.

"Dale, we're home," his mother whispered.

His father woke up slowly, blinking and confused.

This round of chemotherapy had left the burly man weak as a newborn deer. No one hated being feeble more than Dale MacKinnon. When Caleb got out of the truck to help, Dale ignored him and grabbed the handrail instead, each step slow but steady.

His mother, holding his father's jacket, smiled gently. "We're okay here, Caleb. Why don't you put the truck in the garage and get on with your day? We'll see you at dinner. Six, as usual."

Caleb nodded. He parked Dale's ancient Chevy C20 in the garage, climbed into his own Silverado and turned the ignition. The familiar roar of its engine drove away the restless, angry feeling in his chest. He tore down the driveway and headed into town.

California's Central Valley in August—the smell of drought-loosened soil filled Caleb's nose. He slipped his sunglasses out of the glove compartment and slid them on. The metal frames burned his skin. He checked his watch. Three on the dot. Just in time.

He parked across the street from the community college. Cora, in jeans and a white V-neck T-shirt, dashed around his hood and jumped into the cab. She stashed her backpack and gym bag on the floorboard, slid over and gave him a peck on the cheek.

"Hey," he said. A familiar mixture of horniness and contentment settled over him. He felt it whenever she was near.

"Hey, yourself." Her dark hair was in a messy pony-tail and her cheeks were flushed. Besides cherry Chap-Stick, she didn't wear makeup to school. She didn't need to.

"What time do you need to be at work?"

"Five today," she said.

"So where do you want to go?"

She smiled. "Asshole."

"What?" He raised an eyebrow at her. "I just want to know where you want to go."

"You know where."

Twenty minutes away, the almond orchard on the northern edge of his family's property butted up against a wide irrigation channel. Where the guardrail ended, Caleb turned off the asphalt highway and bumped down the sandy road that ran between the water and the end-less rows of trees.

"Are the almonds ready to harvest yet?" Cora asked.

"Almost. Couple weeks."

"After I leave?"

He nodded. He didn't like to think about that.

The water in the channel mirrored the blue-gray sky and the slanting sunlight above. Caleb drove until the highway disappeared in the distance behind them. Privacy wasn't hard to come by in Oleander. All you needed was a truck and a dirt road.

When he was satisfied they were far enough away from passing cars, he turned down one of the shady rows and stopped the car. Here, inside the orchard, the temperature dropped a few degrees, and a thick silence surrounded them as soon as he cut the engine.

She took a little plastic baggie of carrot sticks out of her backpack and munched on them as she scrolled through the texts on her phone.

He took off his seat belt, removed his sunglasses and turned to stare at her. She bit her lip as she texted, smiling to herself. At her hip, he noticed a small hole in her jeans. Her maple-sugar skin shone through the white threads. Through the cotton of her shirt, he could see her bra—pale blue, lacy at the tops of the cups. He felt his body tighten.

After a moment, she looked up. "What?"

"Don't let me rush you or anything."

She turned back to her phone and smiled. "I won't."

Sassy thing. "Whatcha got there?"

She held the bag out to him. "Here. Eat."

He took one. It crunched between his teeth. "Bunny food."

"Ain't I your bunny?"

"You get it on like a bunny."

In response, she turned off her phone, put it back in her bag. With a smile, she took off his hat and put it on the dashboard. He slid out from under the steering column and she climbed into his lap. She hung her arms on his shoulders.

His hand fit perfectly on her hip. "Pictures from the prom came out in the *Oleander Oracle*. Why didn't you ask me? Ain't we going steady?" Even when he teased her, he was careful never to say *boyfriend* or *girlfriend*. Those words always got her hackles up.

"First of all, I couldn't take you. You're old. Ancient."

He took offense at that. "Twenty-two? Since when is that old?"

"Second of all, since when do I have that kind of money to burn? Dress. Flowers. Tickets. To hell with that."

"I would've bought it all for you."

She smirked. "How about you? Did you go to your prom?"

"Sure did. Unforgettable night."

"Who was your date?" she demanded. "She give it up?"

"I'm a gentleman. I don't kiss and tell."

"You're lying. You didn't go."

"I did too. Spiked the punch and everything."

Her brown eyes took on a devilish expression. She reached down and cupped her palm around his hard-on. "When I think about all the places this thing has been, I get a little grossed out."

He kissed her neck and whispered, "You saw my test results. Clean as a whistle, sweetheart. I'm careful."

"All the same." She began to rub him the way he liked.

His shaft twitched against his fly. He flexed his hips, pushing his cock into her hand. "Be nice to me." He licked her earlobe. "This dick's gonna make you feel good this afternoon. Must be all the practice it's had that makes you come so hard."

"Must be." Her eyes fluttered closed and she pressed her lips to his.

Her mouth was cool and sweet, like the carrots she'd been eating. Gently, he pulled her ponytail back, tipping her chin up so that he could deepen their kiss. He slid his tongue against hers. She groaned in her throat and pressed her hands against his chest. In no hurry, he kissed her slow and deep. Her panties got soaked whenever he did it this way.

When he slid his hands underneath her clothes and up the smooth, warm skin of her back, his fingertips glided over the slight ridges of her backbone.

Eyes wide, she broke their kiss and peeled off her T-shirt. He unhooked her pretty blue bra. She leaned forward and slid the straps off her shoulders, releasing the sweet, erotic smell of her skin.

At once, his mouth was on the first nipple he could reach. He sucked it hard and loud as she squirmed in his lap. He twirled her other nipple between the calloused pads of his fingers. She hissed between her teeth. He squeezed her tits in his hands and feasted on the sight of her.

"Jesus Christ, you're beautiful," he murmured.

She kissed him once more and, with an impish smile, slid off his lap, back onto the seat. He watched as she undid his belt buckle and fly. Her nails were neat and clean, no nail polish. But she had blue pen marks all over her hands—notes and random squiggles. He figured she doodled on herself whenever she was bored in class. He'd seen her notebooks—they were pristine.

He lifted his hips and with a mighty yank, she pulled his jeans and boxers down to his knees, releasing his throbbing hard-on. It swung sideways and softly slapped his thigh. Cora made an O with her thumb and forefinger, gripped the base of his cock and gave him a few gentle strokes, milking a clear drop of precome from him as he rested his head back and groaned.

"Do you like it when I go down on you, Caleb?" She tucked a loose strand of black hair behind her ear.

He stroked her bare back. Goose bumps rose on her skin. "Sweetheart, I like everything about you."

She licked her lips until they were slick then dipped her head down over his lap. She popped the crown of his cock between the tight ring of her lips and slid her mouth down his shaft. Heat gripped his body as she squeezed him with her hand, turning her wrist clockwise as she sucked his shaft and tongued the head.

One hand holding the edge of the seat, his other hand resting on the back of her neck, Caleb focused on taking deep, slow breaths. Pleasure coursed through his bloodstream.

In six months, Cora had soaked up everything he taught her. Everything seemed to turn her on. She loved to come. She loved to make him come. She was his most intense wet dream come to life.

"Yeah, girl," he whispered. "Goddamn."

A day after they'd started sleeping together, she'd demanded he drive her all the way up to the clinic in Visalia. "Gimme the industrial-strength birth control," she'd said to the nurse. She insisted Caleb get tested and demanded to see the results. "I'm not getting pregnant like my mom did," she'd told him. "And I'm not getting stuck in godforsaken Oleander for the rest of my life."

He agreed with her wholeheartedly about not making a baby just yet. But when she said things like that—about getting stuck in Oleander, about it being a godforsaken place—he felt a stab of pain in his chest. He didn't feel an excess of love for their hometown, but he didn't hate it either. And he definitely didn't want to see her leave.

Especially not when she did things to him like the thing she was doing right now.

Now at full length, he was long and hard enough that she could wrap both her fists around his shaft as she slurped on the head of his cock. She moved her wrists in such a way that made him see stars—in opposite directions, clockwise and counterclockwise. This move she'd learned on her own—on the Internet or something. He hoped to God she didn't have any other tutor in this subject but him.

"Come on up, sweetheart," he said, stroking her back.

The door of the truck squealed open and *ding*ed until he took the key out of the ignition. She climbed out of the truck, kicked off her sneakers and shimmied out of her jeans and panties. When he reached forward and pulled the elastic gently out of her hair, her dark hair tumbled down. Standing barefoot in the soft dirt, sunlight filtering through the trees onto her naked skin, she looked pure and lovely and perfect.

Confident that none of the farm crews would be coming by this afternoon, Caleb stripped off his clothes too. Shirt, boots, socks, jeans, drawers. He threw everything in the cab of the truck and shut the door with a *bang*, enjoying the look on her face as she ogled him.

His brothers had put a set of weights in the attic of the old farmhouse. Nowadays, Caleb went up there after work to blow off steam, but also for his own vanity—he liked the way Cora looked at him. He liked that he turned her on.

"Come here, cowboy," she said, reaching for him.

Locked in another passionate kiss, she wrapped her legs around his waist and he carried her. Her ass cheeks were firm in his hands. She held on tight as he lowered the tailgate with one hand and pulled a pile of blankets over it to make a soft bed for her. He sat her down on the tailgate and she leaned back on her elbows, her legs hanging off the edge.

A sunbeam shone through a break in the trees, illuminating the piece of heaven between her legs. Shadowed by a small patch of dark hair, her pussy was swollen and lustrous. She flexed her inner muscles and her delicate flesh flared at him in invitation.

He smiled. "Spread your legs."

"You gonna go down?" she whispered.

"You bet your ass I'm gonna go down."

He pulled her to the very edge of the tailgate. She opened her legs and he stared at her sex in the bright sunlight. Delicate caramel lips framed her shell-pink core. He made a V with his thumb and forefinger and gently spread her wide open. He stared at her for a long time, memorizing every velvety fold, the shape of the delicate petal that covered her clit. Gently, he blew on the hot-pink keyhole opening of her pussy. It contracted at once. No wonder she always felt so tight—she was tiny.

"You always stare." She smiled, reached forward and ran her fingers through his hair. Her other hand twirled her nipple. She looked so enticing that in the shade of the tailgate, his cock jerked hard, screaming for attention.

"I'll never stop staring at you. You're gorgeous." He stuck his middle finger in his mouth, wet it and with the barest pressure, skimmed his fingertip along the tender lips of her pussy. She was silky with her own arousal. When he lowered his lips to her and drew circles on her clitoral hood with the tip of his tongue, her toes curled and she moaned, long and deep.

Caleb closed his eyes and fell into a trance. Her smell, her taste, her softness enveloped his senses. He kissed her pussy like he loved kissing her lips—slow and deep. He kept track of the rhythm of her breaths and the slight tremors beneath the surface of her skin.

Her tissues began to swell and her clit, that sweet, vulnerable bundle of nerves, hardened like a BB pellet beneath his tongue. He created a seal over her with his lips and strummed her clit with a steady, unhurried rhythm. Slowly, he slid his index finger deep into her, turned it and drew it out. He repeated the motion, opening her up bit by bit. When her breathing quickened and became shallower, he added his middle finger. She groaned and gripped him like a vise.

When the time was right, he curled his fingertips against her G-spot. Her clit began to vibrate with tension. Her legs trembled. Caleb stole a glance at her—her head thrown back, her lips parted, she was pinching her rosy nipples with the sexual abandon of a woman who knew her body and loved sex. When he felt her take a deep breath and hold it, he unleashed his tongue, savaging her clit until she began to lose control.

At once, Cora threw her arms wide and dug her heels against the edge of the tailgate, lifting her hips so that he could tongue her deeper. When her orgasm broke at last, she shut her eyes and her face twisted up in ecstasy. Hot, sweet liquid filled her pussy, drenching his chin and making it easier for him to piston his fingers in and out of her, extending the climax that shot through her like a rocket.

Breathless, he withdrew, stood up and grabbed his dick. Pressing the head of his cock against her opening, he caught hold of her ankles, spread her legs wide and, with a single snap of his hips, buried his cock inside her as she was still coming.

She wailed. His balls tightened.

"Goddamn it, Caleb," she whimpered, running her hands up and down his chest as he leaned over her. "You feel so fuckin' good."

He couldn't speak. Overwhelmed with lust, he gritted his teeth and stared down at her. She was glistening. Her chest and cheeks were flushed. He smelled clean sweat—hers and his—and the foxy, rich scent of her sex all over his face. All over his cock.

Christ.

He wasn't going to last. They'd made love every day—sometimes twice a day—since February. And still he couldn't seem to control himself when it came to Cora.

Adjusting his footing in the dust, he let go of her ankles, grasped her arms and pulled her up until they were nose to nose. She embraced him and looked deep into his eyes, a mischievous smile on her face.

Her big brown eyes hypnotized him. In the shadows they were black as a bird's. In the sunlight, they turned the color of polished mahogany, like the grandfather clock in his parents' house.

"Hey there," she whispered.

He kissed her tenderly, like she was his delicate treasure, like this was her first kiss. But while he did that, he hammered her pussy with his cock, each brutal thrust digging into her and stretching her beyond what seemed physically possible. He knew he was a big boy—no point pretending he wasn't. But he also knew that she liked it this way. Hard and rough and unforgiving.

She wrapped her smooth legs around his waist, broke their kiss and rested her head against his shoulder. He felt her reach down between their bodies and begin to stroke her clit with her fingertips. Her pussy became impossibly wetter around him.

He licked his lips and whispered in her ear, "You gonna come again?"

"I think so."

Almost delirious from holding back, he grunted and changed his angle so that the top of his cock dragged against the hood of her clit whenever he thrust. Then he grabbed her and began to nuzzle her neck, kissing her sweet spot until she began to whimper.

A minute was all it took. She froze. Suddenly spasms racked her body and her pussy began to convulse wetly around him.

In a heartbeat, Caleb seized her hips, arched his back and came so hard he almost blacked out. His orgasm ran like liquid rapture through his veins, swirled in his balls and shot out of him in long pulls of come.

When it was over, Caleb caught his breath and realized that Cora was kissing him—tiny, tender kisses all over his cheeks and neck.

"Are you all right?" she whispered.

A hot wind rose up in the orchard, stirring the branches and licking the trickle of sweat that ran down his spine. He shivered.

Together, they looked down as he pulled out of her.

Caleb never tired of seeing this. When he withdrew, his come slid out of her in a faint trickle, white against pink. A few drops landed on the ground, darkening the dust at his feet.

He reached for Cora and held her in silence, stroking her long black hair. Back in March, they had made love under these trees in full blossom. White flowers snowed down on them and tangled in Cora's dark hair. Now, all around them, the green branches creaked and swayed in the wind, heavy with ripening fruit.

Every cell in his body screamed, *Don't let her go.*

They lay down in the truck bed together and shared a cigarette. Caleb reached up and plucked an almond from a nearby tree to show her. With his fingers, he stroked the furry green fruit. "This outer part—it's not tasty. We sell it for feed."

"There's a seam there," she said, turning it in the light.

"That's where it splits when the almonds are ready." He cracked open the hull and extracted the pale nutmeat inside. "You want to taste it?"

She frowned at him. "Is it nasty?"

"No, not really. But it needs to ripen and dry out to taste right."

She put it in her mouth. He watched her face as she ate it.

"You're right. It's not bad. But it doesn't taste like an almond. Tastes like...grass." She kissed him and whispered, "Tastes like your come."

He raised an eyebrow at her. "I don't believe you. I think you should do a taste test."

She laughed. "Let me get this straight. I eat a nut...and then you nut, so that I can eat that."

"See, Cora, that's what I like about you. You're one of them classy girls I've heard so much about."

They lay together, joking and horsing around until the alarm on her cell phone went off.

She took some baby wipes out of her gym bag, cleaned up and put on her work uniform, the yellow cotton dress that all the girls at the ice-cream parlor wore. As he polished off her bag of carrots, he watched her brush her hair.

He drove her to work in silence. He couldn't shake the feeling that somewhere there was another timer counting down, another alarm ready to sound. She'd go on to live the rest of her life, and he'd stay put, stuck with a memory of what it felt like to make love to her in an almond orchard, a memory of her in his rearview mirror.

She got out of the truck and, as usual, kissed him through the open driver's side window.

"See you," she said with a smile.

His heart did funny things in his chest as he watched her cross the parking lot and disappear into the shop.

On Saturday, after he helped Clark and Daniel mend fences in the eastern pasture, Caleb washed his truck, took a shower and went to pick up Cora.

Beautiful in the noonday sun, she wore a black tank top, jean shorts and her usual canvas sneakers. When she leaned over and kissed him, she smelled like laundry detergent and shampoo, a sweet herbal scent that made his mouth water.

She was leaving in a week. He was trying not to be sentimental about things, but each time they made love, he began the countdown in his head. Would this be the last time? How much time did he have left with her?

"What do you have planned for us today?" she asked.

"I'm gonna take you on a tour of MacKinnon Ranch."

She smiled. "Ooh, I get a tour?"

"That's right, sweetheart. The twenty-five-cent tour. And afterward, a surprise."

MacKinnon Ranch was five thousand acres, almost eight square miles. When Caleb's maternal grandparents had passed away, their almond orchards were added to the cattle ranch owned by his father's family. His father had razed half of the trees and five years ago had switched to all-natural, grass-fed ranching methods to get a higher price on their beef. Their parcel of land wasn't huge, but Dale's decision had paid off: MacKinnon beef went to gourmet chefs in restaurants all over California. Demand for their product grew stronger each year.

As he drove her around the pastures and along the creek, Caleb answered all of Cora's questions. How big was the herd? "Eight hundred cow-calf pairs." What breed were they? "A cross, Angus-Longhorn." What did they eat? "One hundred percent pasture-raised grass, no grains." Wouldn't the ranch run out of grass? "We rotate pastures." What did the beef taste like? "Like the best meat you've ever sunk your teeth into."

Did he like ranching? "Not really—my brothers like it though."

So what did he like?

He smiled at her. "You know the answer to that, girl."

Following the dirt road that bisected the ranch, he drove until they reached the old aluminum-sided pole barn. He parked behind the barn and grabbed an icy six-pack of beer from the cooler in his truck bed. Cora followed him through a side door.

"What is this place?" she asked as he flipped one of the light switches on the wall.

"We used to keep feed in here. Now we use it for tools." He slid open two dusty windows and a hot cross breeze filled the building. He took her hand and led her past all the junk and tools, up a short flight of wooden steps to the loft.

"Are we gonna have a roll in the hay?" she asked, squeezing his hand.

"Roll, yes. Hay, no."

Caleb's dad stashed old office furniture in the loft, including an ancient leather sofa hidden behind a rolltop desk. Caleb's brothers sometimes slept off benders here, away from their parents or Daniel's wife and kids.

Caleb handed Cora the six-pack. Slung on a rolling office chair were a couple of rain slickers. He shook them out and laid them on the sofa, fleece lining facing up. Then he sat down, looked up at her and patted the space next to him.

Even in the semidarkness, the air inside the barn was dry and hot. Parched, they popped open a couple of beers and drank them down fast. Caleb took off his ball cap, leaned forward and gave her a deep, hungry kiss, plunging his tongue into her ice-cold mouth.

She reached down and peeled his damp T-shirt off his body. He lifted up the front of her tank top, bunched up the fabric in his fingers and stuck it between her teeth, creating a makeshift gag. With a snap of his fingers, he unhooked her bra and shoved the cups upward. Blood pulsing in his ears, he leaned forward and massaged her heavy breasts in his hands, rubbing her nipples with this thumbs as she reached down and stroked the quickly hardening dick in his jeans.

He suckled her hard until her tender nipples were distended and goose bumps rose on her skin. The gag stayed in place as she stared at him with a heavy-lidded gaze that drove him wild. He slid her shoes off, then unbuttoned her shorts and stripped them off her. Too horny to get completely naked, he stood up, undid his belt and lowered his jeans to his knees.

He sat back down on the sofa, slouched low so that his ass was on the edge of the seat.

"Ride me."

Gracefully, she got to her feet, spread her legs and straddled him. When the mouth of her sex opened, he groaned deep in his chest, grabbed the base of his dick and pushed its tip forward until her pussy crowned the head.

Pressing her hands on his sweat-slick chest, she eased her way down, impaling herself on him so deep that he was afraid he might break her. She squeezed him with her inner muscles and he hissed between his teeth. When she did it again, he reached forward and gave each of her nipples a pinch just hard enough to make her squeal.

"I said, ride me. Just like I taught you."

Still gagged, she leaned back, balanced her hands on his knees, and began to raise her hips slowly up and down. Caleb stared at the gorgeous sight of her sex wrapped around his cock, the tight pink tissues stretching to accommodate him, leaving his shaft slick and shiny with her arousal. On the upstroke, her tiny clit protruded outward, like a little pink candy. He licked his thumb, reached forward and grazed it. In response, she squeezed him again, and he grunted like a bear.

"Keep going," he said.

She rode him long and hard, the muscles in her thighs taut and sweat dripping between her breasts.

The barn was sweltering hot, but nothing was hotter than Cora. Caleb watched her, hypnotized. When she leaned back to cant her hips higher, he took mercy on her and plucked the tank top from her mouth. He pulled it over her head, along with her bra.

She took a deep breath and licked her lips.

"You want to say something to me?" he asked.

"Yeah."

"What?"

"I want to tell you that you have a big cock."

He smirked. "Anything else?"

"Yeah. That it feels so good inside me."

With that, he grabbed her. "Stop. Don't move."

Biting her lip, she planted her feet on the ground and stared at him.

He slid down even lower on the sofa. Then he grabbed her hips, held her steady and began to fuck her from below, thrusting his cock up into her while she remained still.

"Oh Jesus," she murmured, closing her eyes.

With each of his thrusts, her tits bounced and her nipples got even harder. She began to sob, lost in the pleasure of their fucking. He reached forward, lubed up the pads of his middle and index fingers in her arousal, and began to draw tiny circles on her clit. She arched her back deeper, licked her lips and let out a long string of swear words. She was so sexy she made him feel unhinged.

"You gonna come for me, sweetheart?" he whispered. "Is this pretty little cunt gonna come?"

"Yes," she whimpered.

Just then, the aluminum walls shook around them. Sunlight flooded the interior of the barn as the large double doors swung open.

Cora and Caleb froze, trembling, as they listened to the voices rising from below.

"Where is it?"

"The post driver? Back next to those crates somewhere."

"I see the farm jack."

Caleb shut his eyes and swore silently. All three of his brothers: Dean, Daniel and Clark.

"Who left these windows open?" Daniel said. He shut them with a bang.

"Is someone in here? Caleb?" called Dean.

Quickly but carefully, Cora slid off.

Caleb pulled up his jeans and tucked his throbbing hard-on into his boxers as gingerly as he could. "Yeah, I'm in here!" he shouted, zipping up. His voice caught in his throat.

Covering up her breasts, Cora stared up at him, eyes wide.

"Don't worry," Caleb whispered, getting his T-shirt back on.

"What the hell are you doing up there?" Clark said. Tools clanged around in the corner.

"Hang on," Caleb called out. He wiped his forehead with the back of his hand, got his hat back on, and dashed down the steps.

Cora got dressed in a hurry and stayed where she was, inching up against the wall where no one would see her unless they went upstairs.

From the expressions on their faces, it took his brothers all of ten seconds to figure out what he'd been up to in the loft. Dean, the eldest, just smiled, smacked him on the shoulder and walked back outside. But Clark and Daniel were ready to give him hell for bringing a girl up into the old pole barn. It didn't matter that they'd all done the same thing at one time or another—their sole purpose in life was to make fun of him, and they lived lives rich with purpose.

"So, have you got the post driver, Clark?" said Daniel, nice and loud for the benefit of the unseen girl in the loft.

"Sure do, Dan!" said Clark, smiling.

"Great!" said Caleb, trying to herd them out. "I'll close up for you on your way out."

"Thanks, Caleb!" Clark said. "Hey, Dan, remember when Caleb was twelve and he used to sneak up here by himself to jack off?"

Caleb shoved Clark into a pile of cardboard boxes.

Clark stifled a laugh as he got to his feet.

"Oh, man," Daniel said, "he couldn't get his hands on porno so what did he used to use?"

Overloud, Clark said, "Our mom's old JCPenney catalog. He'd yank it to the old ladies' nightgown section."

"Remember when he tried to deny it? We showed him that the pages were stuck together."

"Motherfuckers, I swear," Caleb hissed.

Laughing, Daniel and Clark left the barn and started to pull the doors closed. "Dinner's in twenty minutes, Caleb!"

"Tacos tonight! Don't be late!"

"Yum! Tacos!"

Caleb rubbed the bridge of his nose as he listened to his brothers' laughter fading away in the distance. Once again, he felt the particular pain of being born not only the youngest, but also an "oops", as in, "Oops, we had a baby ten years after our last one". Caleb sometimes felt like he had five parents instead of two.

He climbed back up the steps to where Cora was waiting on the sofa, completely dressed, with her legs crossed. Her cheeks were flushed, but she was covering her smile with her hand and shaking her head slowly.

"Oh my God," she said, laughing.

"Sorry about that." He sat down heavily next to her and took a gulp of beer. He'd gone half-staff, but his balls ached like they'd been stomped on. "They can be assholes sometimes."

She leaned over, wrapped her arms around his shoulders and kissed his cheek. "It's all right. And I completely understand. Some of those JCPenney models *are* kinda hot."

He kissed her back, glad that she was a good sport about it all. The sun was still out, but no one would be in the orchard this late. They could still finish what they started. "How about a drive?"

"Actually," she said, raising her eyebrows, "how about some tacos?"

He frowned. "Are you kidding?"

"No, I'm serious. I'd like to meet your family. Could I have dinner with you guys?"

There was always enough food to go around, even when unexpected guests showed up at the table. But he'd never brought a girl to dinner before. And none of his brothers had ever brought a Mexican girl to the house. Unexpected anxieties crept up on him. "After all that? You still want to meet my family? My douche-bag brothers?"

"Of course I do." She stood up and straightened her tank top. "I'm not embarrassed. We're adults. We don't have anything to be ashamed of." She smiled sheepishly. "Although, if it'd been your mom, I might've shriveled up and died."

He turned his ball cap backwards, reached forward and wrapped his arms around her waist, resting his forehead against her warm stomach. After a long time, he said, "You know, sometimes I forget."

"Forget what?"

"How mature and smart you are."

"I'm not that smart." She stroked his cheeks. "But I *am* pretty hungry."

It shouldn't have surprised Caleb that his family loved Cora. Brainy, articulate, polite—she was great. His father asked about her plans and she talked about her scholarship to Brown and how she was leaving in a couple of days. She fielded all of his brothers' stupid-ass questions and even helped his mother and sister-in-law clear the dishes. Daniel's kids were on their best behavior. Not used to seeing a young woman at the table,

Caleb's nephew Derek stared at Cora with eyes big as platters, falling irrevocably in love with her as soon as she said hello to him. Caleb smiled, knowing the feeling all too well.

Four-year-old Derek was also the only one brave enough to broach the topic of race.

"Cora?"

"Yes, Derek?"

"Are you a Mexican?"

"My parents are. But I was born here, so I'm an American."

"Oh." He paused. "Do you speak Spanish?"

"I sure do."

"Cool."

And that was that.

After dinner, Caleb drove Cora to her grandmother's house, but not before she made him pull over by the side of the road. In a breathless rush, they finished each other off in the cab of his truck, him going down on her until she screamed hoarsely and came in a juicy shudder, her riding him until he exploded hard enough to hit his head on the back window, rattling his brains.

He dropped her off. She got out of the truck and, as usual, kissed him goodbye through the driver's side window.

"See you." She smiled and walked into the darkened house.

He watched her and realized that one more day with her was now gone forever.

The week sped past. Cora finished her classes at the community college and got her final grades: two As and an A minus. For her last days in Oleander, she packed up her things and spent as much time as possible with her grandmother. Caleb had to content himself with seeing her for a couple of hours in the middle of the day.

Both of them knew their time together was coming to an end, and the sex reflected that—they fucked each other senseless whenever they could. Caleb expressed worries he'd chafe his dick on her. Cora said she had moments where she thought she could still feel him inside her, like some kind of bizarre phantom limb. They'd had a good laugh at that.

On her last day at the ice-cream parlor, her coworkers threw her a party with balloons and secret vodka-and-lemon-sorbet shots in the back room. Smiling, she showed Caleb the card they'd all signed. On the front was a picture of a shirtless cowboy. Inside, the inscription said, *Save a Horse and Ride Him Instead.*

As Caleb alternated between his family's ranch and the Hughes ranch, he felt hollow inside. Cora had made him feel grounded and alive for the first time in his life. The universe had played yet another sick joke on him.

He'd found the perfect woman, with one fatal flaw—she wasn't his. She'd never said she was. She'd take off for college and he'd be back to being a lonely bastard, chasing the wrong women. More one-night stands. The same old miseries, worsened by the knowledge that life didn't have to suck so hard.

On the evening before Caleb was supposed to drive her to the airport, Cora called him.

"My grandmother wants to meet you. She's making a special dinner for us. Come over to the house." She paused. "Um, you should wear something nice."

"But doesn't your grandmother only speak Spanish?"

"I'll translate. You just be your charming self, *güero*."

He knew that word. White boy.

Caleb ironed a black button-down shirt and took a pair of new boots down off the shelf in his closet. He showered, shaved and combed his hair. A pair of stiff dark jeans and a new white cowboy hat, and Caleb was as dressed up as he ever got.

Before he left for Cora's, his father stopped him in the living room. In his Barcalounger, Dale put down his newspaper and gave a low whistle. "Look at you, kiddo. Sharp."

"Cora's grandmother invited me for dinner."

"That right?" He nodded slowly. "Well, don't do anything that'll embarrass our family."

Caleb smiled. "I won't, Dad."

As he passed the kitchen, his mother shoved something into his hands—a cellophane bag tied with ribbon.

"I baked cookies," she said. "You should never go to dinner at someone's house without a gift. It's rude."

"Oh," he said, way out of his element. "Thanks."

"I like that girl, you know." There was a weird glassy look in his mother's eyes. "Oh, Caleb. I hate to see you hurting."

He'd tried his best not to sulk. Apparently he'd failed. "I'm doing all right. We knew it was coming."

"I know, I know. Never mind me." She turned and walked back into the kitchen, sniffling a little. "I just want to see you happy, is all."

For the first time that he could remember, Caleb parked his truck right in front of Cora's grandmother's house. The smell of home cooking filled the air. Cora answered the door wearing a starched white blouse, dark skirt, dark tights and black shoes. Her long hair was coiled into an old-fashioned swirly thing on the back of her head.

With a sideways glance toward the kitchen, she kissed his cheek. "Not a word about what I'm wearing. Not a single word."

"I wasn't going to say anything, Sister Cora," he whispered.

She pinched his ass hard enough for him to stifle a yelp.

The living room was sparsely furnished but immaculately clean. As he hung up his hat, Caleb realized that there was, in fact, a sheathed machete in Cora's grandmother's hat rack, at the ready for castrating any man who threatened her granddaughter's honor. Caleb gulped like a cartoon character.

A little iron-gray-haired woman dressed identically to Cora stepped out of the kitchen. Caleb shook the old lady's hand as Cora introduced him as her *amigo*. Not *novio*. He knew both words—*friend* and *boyfriend*—two very different things.

Though Caleb had been expecting a formal meal, he felt welcome at their small, cozy table. After she said a blessing, Cora's grandmother served Cora's favorite dish—*birria*, goat stew.

She and Cora watched with anticipation as the *güero* examined his food. Would he be too squeamish? Or would he eat it? Caleb smiled. He would, and he'd enjoy it too—it tasted like lamb. Along with vegetables from their garden and fresh homemade tortillas, the stew was one of the best things he'd ever had.

With Cora translating, Caleb talked about his time as a ranch hand in Montana and Nevada. He asked Cora's grandmother questions about her life in Jalisco.

Before he'd died of a heart attack, Cora's grandfather had been a farm worker in the sugar-cane fields there. The machete by the door was in fact his cane knife. Cora's grandmother had brought it with her to the United States; it made her feel like he was always looking over the family.

Over cups of dark coffee, the cookies his mother had made and a sweet custard called *jericalla*, Caleb tried out the phrases he'd been practicing.

"Gracias por su hospitalidad, Señora Gomez." Thank you for your hospitality. *"Estoy muy orgulloso de Cora."* I'm very proud of Cora.

Smiling, Cora's grandmother said in halting English, "And thank you for making my granddaughter so happy. I'm proud of her too."

Between them, Cora blushed like a stoplight.

After the meal, Caleb parked his truck around the block and waited. The minutes stretched out into an eternity. A half hour after he'd bid Cora and her grandmother goodbye and pretended to drive home, his phone buzzed with a text.

She's asleep. Window by the tomatoes.

He took off his white hat and left it on the seat. Saying a silent prayer of apology to Cora's grandfather, he crept along the side of the house and used an old potting bench to boost himself up into the open window where Cora waited for him in bed.

Shelves stuffed with books lined the walls of her bedroom. A large rolling suitcase stood by the door. A little ceramic nightlight shaped like an angel glowed on her bedside table.

"You clean up nice, MacKinnon," she whispered between the hot kisses he dropped on her lips as he stumbled to get out of his clothes. "And you said such nice things to my grandma. She loves you."

How about you? Do you love me?

"Stop talking and find something to bite on, girl," he said.

She stifled a giggle and welcomed him under the covers. She was naked and warm. Her hair was loose, freed from its Victorian cinnamon roll. "Jesus Christ, your feet are cold," she hissed.

"All the blood's somewhere else." He hid behind his jokes—they were all he had left to protect himself.

She kissed him—long, openmouthed kisses without end. He drank her in, his tongue searching her mouth, thirsty for more. She reached down and wrapped her sweet little fingers around his shaft, pumping slowly with the overhand grip she knew he liked.

He felt himself dissolving into her faded flower-print sheets, his nerve endings humming with pleasure. He trailed kisses down to her tits and suckled her nipples until they were rosy and tender.

He caught his breath and rested his burning cheek against her breast.

"I can't believe I'm leaving tomorrow," she whispered, combing her fingers through his hair.

He said nothing. Heartbreak lodged in his chest like lead shot.

She said softly, "So this is it. The last time."

Tell her you love her. Ask her to stay.

"Let's make it good, then," he said.

In her tiny twin bed, Caleb went down on her slowly, his cast-iron erection buried in the sheets. In the semidarkness, he knew every tiny ridge and silky tissue of her pussy as though he were the cartographer who'd drawn the map. With surgical precision, he brought her to the brink and held back, again and again, completely in control of her body. When he let her come at last, the orgasm was enormous; her face contorted in ecstasy, she shuddered silently against his lips. The air in the room grew rich with the smell of sex.

Both the bed and the ancient wooden floor were squeaky as hell. Careful not to make a sound, Caleb raised himself on his arms and looked down at Cora. In six months, she'd gone from a scared, nervous girl to a confident woman who knew what turned her on.

With a smile, she reached down and guided him into her body. He slid his hips forward slowly until he was planted inside her as far as he could go. When she squeezed him, the exquisite agony wrenched a groan from his chest. He began his long, slow ride.

"Are you gonna remember me?" he murmured.

She ran her hands up and down his abs and chest and rested her palms on his biceps, stroking his muscles with her fingers. "What do you think?"

"I think you'll forget. When you start dating out there. When you get a boyfriend."

"I won't." He watched her lick her lips and gasp as he thrust, digging the head of his cock against her smooth inner walls. She whispered, "But sometimes I think you're already forgetting me. Even when we do this."

Anger rushing to the forefront, he froze, grabbed her shoulders and lifted her up to look her in the eyes. "That's bullshit and you know it. I'm fucking crazy about you."

Her eyes were plaintive, dark as a night without stars. "Don't say it. Please. I can't hear you say it."

Before all the words he'd regret came spilling out of his big mouth, he put his hand on the back of her neck and crushed his lips against hers. He swallowed her whimpers and pulled her body against his until she was sitting in his lap, her legs wrapped cross-legged around his hips. He arched his back and thrust into her again and again, the familiar heat rushing through his veins, his orgasm gathering like a rainstorm ready to break.

As much as he wanted to hold on to her, how could he ask her to stay? Her years of hard work had paid off—a full-ride scholarship to an Ivy League university. People in their town rarely went to college, much less a big, fancy one back East. She was making good on promises she'd made to herself and the woman who'd raised her. He sure as shit wasn't going to stand in her way.

He broke their kiss. "You ready to fly, sweetheart?"

There were tears in her eyes. It was the first time he'd seen her cry since their first night together. "Yes."

Caleb MacKinnon didn't know how to do much. He knew how to rebuild an engine. He knew how to get a boom shaker working again. And he knew how to make Corazón Gomez come like a wildcat.

With his fingers, his cock and his extensive knowledge of her body, he gave her one last climax. Her fingertips dug into his back, and she came so hard and so long he thought he'd broken her.

Giving her nipples a final suckle, he flipped her onto her back and fucked her deep, trying to tell her with his body what he couldn't tell her with words. His orgasm exploded out of him like a bull breaking a gate. It wasn't pretty. Cora reached up and frantically clapped her hands over his mouth as he grunted and flooded her with come.

Sleep threatened to drag him under, but Cora herded him out of her bed. "My grandma wakes up early. You can't stay."

"What's she gonna do? Throw you out of the house?" he said. But he got up anyway. Uncoordinated and groggy, he got dressed and climbed out of the open window. She kissed him over the windowsill as he stood on the rickety potting bench outside.

"What time do you want me to come get you tomorrow?" he whispered.

"Seven."

"Okay. I'll be here."

Taxis and airport shuttles jockeyed for space at the curb as Caleb parked his truck in the white zone. He got out, lifted Cora's suitcase out of the truck bed and set it down next to her on the sidewalk.

"Do you have your ticket?" he asked.

"Yup."

"What time does your plane leave?"

"Soon. But I still have to check in." She double-checked her ticket, her wallet, her purse and all the zippers on her suitcase. She wasn't taking much because she didn't have much to take. Even so, she looked a little overwhelmed.

As she stood there reviewing her stuff, he memorized the sight of her: sundress, sandals, braided dark hair. The long, hot drive had left her cheeks rosy.

Cars honked. A porter pushed a cart loaded with luggage. All around them, people rushed to their destinations.

She glanced up at him and gave him a distracted hug. "Okay. I'd better go," she said, already turning away.

He grabbed her shoulders and held her still. "Whoa. Slow down, Ivy League."

Tipping his head so that he wouldn't blind her with the brim of his cowboy hat, Caleb kissed her. Her lips were soft and still tasted like the Cherry Coke he'd bought her at a gas station in Valencia. Not caring that they were in a public place, he opened his mouth and gave her a little tongue. She laughed against his mouth, stepped in between his boots and gave him a real hug.

"I'm going to miss you," he said.

She pulled away a half inch and looked into his eyes. "Don't. Don't miss me." He could tell she was struggling to stay tough. He didn't want to see her cry again. "We talked about this," she whispered. "I don't want a long-

distance relationship. Here's where we have to say goodbye."

He nodded and stole another kiss.

She pulled away again. "I'm serious, Caleb. You go
out with other girls. I'll go out with...my textbooks. End
of story. Period."

He nodded again and smiled. "Text me when you ar-
rive, okay?"

"You son of a bitch, are you even listening to me?"

Her lips were too sweet. He kissed her again. "You
gonna text me or what?"

She sighed. "Fine."

He lowered his lips to her ear. "You gonna send me
dirty pictures?"

"Oh my God. Goodbye, MacKinnon."

"What's the word? Your *panocha*? Yeah. Send me a
picture of that."

She smiled at last. "Stupid ass."

One final kiss and she slipped out of his arms.

Tonight, with the help of his brothers back in Oleander, Caleb was going to drink himself numb. But right
now, watching Cora wheel her suitcase into the terminal, he wanted to feel it all: anger that she had to go, de-
spair that he couldn't keep her and happiness that she
was leaving to pursue her dreams—none of which in-
cluded life in a Podunk town with him.

Cora looked over her shoulder. She stepped inside, nodded at him and mouthed the words, *See you.*

"See you," he said aloud.

With a parting smile, she turned away as the glass doors shut behind her.

CHAPTER THREE

Romeo

Courage is being scared to death...and saddling up anyway.

—JOHN WAYNE

Cora was sleeping facedown on her open statistics textbook, her nose wedged into the crack, when the buzz of her cell phone woke her up. She squinted at the screen. Almost one a.m. Only one person ever texted her this late at night.

What are you wearing?

She smiled as she slid her textbook out of the way. With a yawn, she stretched out on the top bunk, delighting in the juicy feeling of unfurling her spine and cracking her vertebrae like knuckles. She lay back on her pillow and thought for a moment before texting back.

A frown of indignation.

The reply came back immediately. *Easy, Ivy League. You and them 25-cent words. Hold on.*

She stifled a laugh as another text came through.

Just looked that word up. Anger and annoyance, my ass. You like it when I text you late at night. That's when you're the horniest.

Cora rolled her eyes. *Speak for yourself, cowboy. Late at night is when I study.*

You studying now?

Her fingers flew over her phone. *No. Obviously I'm wasting time texting you. What are you doing home on a Friday night, anyway? Shouldn't you be drinking at the Silver Spur or hanging out with the other delinquents?*

Who said I was home?

She felt a flash of annoyance. *So where are you?*

There was a long pause before he replied. *Outside your window.*

She laughed. *Don't make horror-movie jokes. I'm alone here and you know how freaked out I get.*

You ain't alone. Go to your window.

Fuck you, Caleb! If you insist on freaking me out I will end this conversation right now.

Don't freak out. Just look. Please.

"Stupid ass," Cora whispered, unsure of whether she was directing the insult at Caleb or at herself.

In a huff, she climbed down the ladder of her bunk bed, zipped up her pink hoodie and shuffled over to the window. She pulled up the blinds and looked outside.

The night sky was black and starless as tar. Everything on the ground was covered in a thick layer of white snow, a sight that still surprised and delighted Cora, who had only seen snow for the first time a couple of months ago. "What am I supposed to be seeing?" she said aloud, squinting.

A few sets of footprints crossed the quad like the snail trails, but no one was out. Only the crazy or the drunk would venture out on a cold night like this.

Cora's phone buzzed. She glanced at it.

Can you see me?

She was confused. From her fourth-story window, she could hardly see anything but snow. Then she spotted something that almost made her drop her phone.

Within the perfectly round halo of light from a streetlamp stood a tall figure with a duffel bag slung over his shoulder. He was wearing jeans, a dark jacket and a black cowboy hat. When he waved, the screen of a cell phone created an eerie blue arc that seemed to hang in the air.

Surprise and trepidation coursed through Cora's bloodstream in two huge waves. Despite the radiator in her room, her fingers went cold as she sent him one more text.

You crazy bastard.

Frantic, she stumbled to the bathroom, brushed her teeth and dragged a comb through her slept-on hair. When she looked in the mirror, she saw only pasty skin and bloodshot eyes. She sighed, took out a tube of Chap-Stick and smeared it on, hoping that by some cherry-flavored miracle Caleb had become severely nearsighted in the six months since she'd seen him.

"Friends, right? We're just friends," she whispered to herself. It was a lie as bald-faced as she was.

She went downstairs. A couple of students snoozed or chatted quietly in the study lounge. Cora glanced through the window at the figure waiting just outside the door.

Tall and solid, Caleb stood with one hand in the pocket of his jeans and one hand holding his duffel bag. His boots crunched over the thin crust of fresh snow on the front steps, and he looked wild-eyed and out of his element. Cora took a deep breath and opened the door.

At once, Caleb dropped his duffel bag and gave her a bear hug. When he smashed her face up against his Carhartt jacket, the coldness of his body seeped through her Hello Kitty flannel pajamas into her skin. In the crush of his embrace, Cora wondered if her heat passed through his clothes and into his skin.

As if he could read her thoughts, he squeezed her harder, making her squeak involuntarily, like a dog toy.

She could feel the hot staring of the other students, so she pulled away and looked up at him.

Those eyes. Jesus H. Christ. Green as sea glass with pupils rimmed in gold. The tip of his nose was red. He sniffled. For some reason this pinched at her heart—her big, tough cowboy had a little cold.

No, she thought to herself, *not* your *cowboy.*

"Hey." He leaned forward and kissed her forehead with cold lips. "Happy Valentine's Day."

"Why didn't you tell me you were coming?"

"I wanted to surprise you. Or embarrass you if you were on a date, which"—he looked her up and down—"doesn't seem to be the case."

She winced and let go. "These days I only date my statistics textbook."

"That douche bag? I'll kill him. Where is he?" Caleb said with a fake sneer. Even though he was joking, his possessiveness made Cora swallow down the bubble of wishful thinking that appeared in her throat.

"Upstairs in my bed," she said. "Come on."

As Caleb showered in the men's bathroom, Cora made up her roommate's empty bunk bed with spare blankets and a pillow. She dug out some cold medicine and heated up the electric kettle. Then she went to the bathroom to wash her mug and spoon.

She scrubbed the coffee stains out of the mug and tried to gather her thoughts.

Why is he here? What does he want?

It had been so long since they'd seen each other in person. Cora had no other family but her grandmother, who couldn't drive. Caleb—her not-boyfriend, then or now—had volunteered to drive Cora and see her off at the airport in Los Angeles, three hours from their dusty hometown in California's Central Valley. That was back in August.

Against her better judgment, they'd stayed in contact, texting each other at least once a day. And there had been those long phone conversations that Cora had to take in the stairwell where her roommate couldn't hear the words that Caleb wanted her to say.

Tonight, Cora could tell something was wrong with Caleb—his green eyes were ghosted and restless.

Is he sick? Is he getting enough rest?

She knew his dad had passed away a couple months earlier, but he didn't like to talk about it.

Should I bring that up?

She dried off the mug with some paper towels. When she looked up, she almost screamed in surprise.

Caleb stood behind her, a towel wrapped around his lean hips, her bottle of strawberry body wash in his hand. She could see the muscles in his chest and his washboard abs, still beaded with water.

"Holy hell!" Her heart was pounding. "You were supposed to go to the men's bathroom. I told you. Downstairs, one floor down."

He looked stunned, Bambi in the headlights. "I guess...I guess I didn't hear the downstairs part."

"Jesus! Caleb!" she said, exasperated.

Thousands of miles from home, both feeling a little lost, they looked at each other in the mirror.

"Oops." He cracked a smile.

They began to laugh.

Caleb put an arm around her waist and kissed her cheek. She'd always thought he was the most handsome when he smiled. He was warm from his hot shower. She closed her eyes and leaned back against his hard, solid chest, enjoying his heat.

"Let me get out of here before I get you in trouble," he whispered.

"My room is unlocked," she said. "I'll be there in a minute."

"Where's your roommate anyway?"

"Romantic Valentine's Day weekend. She'll be gone until Monday."

"That so?" Caleb raised an eyebrow at her.

"Yup."

He walked out of the restroom and Cora caught herself checking out his behind, perfect and tight and just round enough to ruin her for all other behinds for the rest of her life.

Caleb dried off and got into a clean T-shirt and boxers. He dove into the bed and covered himself up in an attempt to hide the enormous erection he'd gotten as soon as Cora leaned up against him in the bathroom.

She hadn't reciprocated his kiss or even touched him. But her deep brown eyes when she looked at him, the baby-soft skin on her cheek when he kissed her, the sweetness of her smile when she laughed—everything about her conspired to make the blood in his body rush south in a hurry. In spite of ample opportunities to mess around with other girls since Cora left town, he hadn't slept with anyone else. None of them appealed to him anymore. But now that Cora was near, his body throbbed like an exposed nerve.

She came in a minute later, her cheeks glowing. She closed the door behind her, poured him a cup of hot chamomile tea and gave him some cold medicine without his asking for it.

"I've got the radiator on. Are you warm enough?" she asked.

After a six-hour flight and three hours slogging around in the snow looking for her, Caleb was fading fast. The blanket and pillow, and now even his own skin, smelled like her—fresh and sweet like strawberries. In spite of his exhaustion, his cock was still heavy and rigid, with no intention of standing down. He put the pills in his mouth, took a long drink and put the mug on the bedside table.

"I'm plenty warm," he said.

She turned off the lamp and began to climb up into the top bunk.

"Cora. Wait."

In the dark, he listened to her, frozen on the ladder, breathing.

"Lie down with me," he whispered.

"Caleb," she said softly. "We can't. We shouldn't."

He liked his name on her lips so much that he ignored the impatience in her voice. "I won't try anything."

She *pfft'*d.

"Please," he said.

"These beds are really narrow. We'll be squished together."

"Cora." He could hear his own voice beginning to slur. He'd never been on a plane before. Everything in this place was new and strange—except for her.

After a moment of introspection in the dark, she climbed back down, lifted the blanket and slid in next to him.

In the narrow bunk, he spooned her, wrapping his arms around her just underneath her breasts. As if it were the most natural thing in the world, she bent her legs, and he tucked his knees behind hers. His rigid cock rested snugly against her lower back.

"Whoa, there," she said softly, jerking forward.

He held her tightly, not letting her wiggle loose. *Fuck, she feels like heaven,* he thought. "It'll go away. Eventually."

She sighed and stopped fidgeting, but she still felt skittish in his arms. He tightened his grip and nuzzled the side of her neck, a sweet spot that he knew either put her to sleep or made her wet, depending on how he did it. The tension drained slowly from her body like moonshine from a still.

They were quiet for a long time. Caleb tried to ignore how right she felt in his arms.

"You know," she said quietly, "we've never actually *slept* together."

Caleb opened his eyes in the dark and blinked. The cold medicine was beginning to cross his wires a little. "Really? Never?"

"Maybe a nap by the creek, but that was only an hour or so," she said.

He smiled. "I remember that afternoon." He tried not to nudge her with his dick.

"Seems a long time ago," she murmured.

"Yeah."

A long pause. "So...why are you here anyway?" she asked.

The big question. He couldn't answer it. Not tonight, anyway.

"I'll tell you tomorrow."

She wrapped her arms around his and her girlish sigh dug right into his heart. The last thing he remembered before exhaustion dragged him under was the sound of her deep breathing, soft and even. As close as they were, and as worn out as he was, she could have been breathing for them both.

Cora woke up from the deepest sleep she'd had in months. Buried in blankets and pillows, she had to wiggle her way free. Sunlight filled the dorm room from between the curtains.

She looked at the digital clock on her desk—9:48.

The door opened and in stepped the cowboy.

"Morning, sunshine," Caleb said, taking off his hat.

She looked up at him. Without his hat, his disheveled dark blond hair made his green eyes look almost feral. He put down the coffee and donuts he was carrying and took off his jacket. Tall and toned in his snug-fitting Henley and jeans, he was everything attractive to her about men.

He leaned down and gave her a kiss on the cheek, bringing with him the smell of fresh coffee. As he stood up straight in the small dorm room, with its pink daisy bedspreads and twinkle lights, he looked as out of place as a longhorn in a nail salon.

"My smokes are in the top drawer of the desk, if you want one." She rubbed her eyes.

"No thanks. Gave it up." He sat down at the foot of the bed. "What did you give me last night? It put me down like an elephant dart."

"Just a little nighty-night cold medicine. How do you feel?"

"A thousand times better." He looked at her intently. "Listen. How long will it take you to shower and pack an overnight bag?"

"What? Why?"

"I've got a surprise for you." He leaned back on his arms and the caps of muscle on his shoulders flexed forward. "My brother Dean is working tonight. Madison Square Garden. I got us tickets. What d'you say?"

She sat up. "I say you're a nutjob. I've got a huge project due on Monday."

"And if I know you correctly, you've been done with it for at least three weeks."

He always had her number. "But...I have to review the data," she said weakly.

"You can review it on the train. We've got a three-hour ride."

"Caleb! I can't just waltz off to the rodeo."

He smiled, unfazed by her resistance. "You can and you will. With me. And we're gonna have a hell of a time."

She groaned.

"Come on, Corazón. Sweetheart. Do it for me." He flashed her that infuriatingly handsome smirk. "It'll be fun."

The express train sped along Connecticut's wintry coast. During a stop in New London, Caleb stood up to stretch his legs. When he came back, a clean-cut cadet from the Coast Guard Academy was sitting across the aisle from Cora, chatting with her and being far too friendly for Caleb's taste. The cowboy eyed the sailor and vice versa until the cadet, knowing he'd been outclassed, bid Cora a polite goodbye and cleared out.

Cora smiled so sweetly at Caleb as he took his seat that he knew something was wrong. "What?"

"What do you mean 'what'? I've never seen you act that way."

"What way?"

"Like a snorting bull. That guy was just asking me about my laptop. He wanted to know if I liked it because he was thinking of getting one for himself."

"No doubt he wanted to get one for himself," Caleb said, looking her up and down, "but he wasn't thinking about no laptop."

She rolled her eyes and turned back to her work as the train picked up speed again. Caleb wanted to talk to her some more, but he knew she had to work. Instead, he stared out the window at the steel-gray sky and the cold land spread out beneath it.

As she typed, Cora's elbow rubbed gently against his bicep, making the muscle twitch and tingle for more contact. He could smell her freshly shampooed hair. In the warm train car, her cheeks were flushed like pink roses. She was dressed in a soft wool sweater that rode her curves and jeans that hugged her little heart-shaped ass.

God, how could he blame the cadet? She was beautiful. Who wouldn't want a chance with her?

His mind wandered to a night a few weeks before she'd left.

Cora had been closing up the ice-cream parlor when he stopped by after everyone else had left. Without a word, she led him into the back room, lifted up her dress and pulled down her panties. He took her hard against the metal shelves filled with sleeves of sugar cones and huge jars of devil-red maraschino cherries. They came in complete silence, seconds apart, his heart beating so hard that he thought he was going to die of a heart attack, buried to the hilt inside a girl whose blood ran as hot as his.

The train pulled into Penn Station a little after three thirty. Caleb held Cora's hand and led her the short walk to the Hotel New Yorker, where his brother Dean had reserved a room for them. Anticipation humming in his veins, Caleb was herding her quickly to their room when he looked up and spotted a couple of familiar faces.

"MacKinnon!"

The wiry fellow by the elevator felt no qualms about yelling out Caleb's name as though they were standing in the middle of a cow pasture in Oleander and not in the crowded lobby of a New York hotel.

"Jesus Christ," said Caleb, putting down his bag. "Decker Daniels."

As the bull rider caught up Caleb's hand in an iron grip, Decker's girl came out from behind him.

Caleb looked up in surprise. "Andie? That you?"

Back home, the ranch foreman had kept his daughter in secondhand dresses and ratty coveralls. But the woman standing before them was as resplendent as a butterfly, a glitzy cowgirl in rhinestones and fancy leather boots. Her hair and makeup were camera perfect.

She leaned forward and gave him a peck on the cheek. Caleb felt Cora stiffen beside him.

"Been a long time, Caleb," Andie said.

"She cleans up good, don't she?" Decker wrapped his arm around her waist. He eyed Cora. "Who's this, now?"

Caleb squeezed Cora's hand as he pulled her forward gently. "Cora Gomez. Studies at Brown. But she's from Oleander too." He turned to her. "Decker here is a bull rider. He's ranked eighth in the world. Andie's his fiancée."

Cora's eyes flickered to the giant diamond ring on Andie's hand.

"College girl," said Decker with admiration. "What are you studying?"

"Business." Cora fidgeted with her wool sweater. Caleb had never known Cora to fidget with anything.

Decker nodded. "Good for you. Should be a fun event tonight. Fresh riders, a shitload of new bulls. And the New York crowd cheers louder than anywhere else. How do you like bull riding, Cora?"

"I don't know. It's my first time."

Andie and Decker looked at her and smiled in unison.

"You'll love it," said Andie.

"We're heading upstairs for a spell." Caleb felt his heartbeat quicken at the prospect. "Where are you two off to?"

"I have to get to the Garden," said Decker. "Your brother's there now. We've got some promotional stuff to do. Interviews and photos. The event starts at seven."

"I was going to see him off and kill time until then," said Andie.

"Uh..." Cora let go of Caleb's hand, "...Andie, is it? I know I just met you, but...could I ask you a favor?"

"What's up?" asked Andie.

Caleb turned to Cora. "I thought you wanted to freshen up. Upstairs." *With me. Naked.*

"That's just it," said Cora. "I don't have anything to wear tonight. I was wondering if you could help me out."

Andie's eyes lit up and she bounced up and down on the balls of her feet, making Decker's eyes bug out of his head.

"Oh, honey. Are you kidding? I got tons of clothes upstairs. You're a little slender thing, but we're bound to find something that fits you." Andie turned to Decker. "Why don't you take Caleb with you to see his brother while Cora and I doll up?"

With a smile, Cora picked up Caleb's duffel bag. "You two go on. We'll meet you there."

Caleb watched as the two girls headed for the elevator, already chatting like best friends. He suppressed a groan.

Decker slapped Caleb on the back hard enough to rattle his teeth. "Orders is orders, kid. Come on."

Andie stripped off Cora's coat and gave her a gentle shove into the restaurant where Caleb was waiting at the bar.

"I'll see you up at our seats." Andie turned and left to meet Decker in the VIP area, her perfect brown curls bouncing underneath a bedazzled white cowboy hat.

Cora folded her arms and glanced at her own reflection in the plate-glass window that separated the bar from the hostess stand.

Andie was much taller than Cora, so her breathtaking array of jeans and flashy western shirts hadn't fit. Undaunted, Andie had dug a hot-pink strapless minidress out of the bottom of her suitcase and made Cora put it on.

"But I don't have a strapless bra," Cora had protested.

"You've got great nineteen-year-old boobs, though. That's more important." With determination, Andie had yanked the fabric up and given Cora's bottom a playful spank.

Here in public, Cora felt naked times ten. She thought that a glamorous cowgirl makeover would make her feel confident, not exposed. Nothing covered her bare shoulders except for the thick mass of dark waves that Andie had steam-curled into her hair. In addition to the tiny dress, Cora wore a big, braided Western-style belt, a bejeweled belt buckle and brown leather cowboy boots that fit perfectly. She blinked but fought the urge to rub her eyes. Andie had done her makeup too—glittery eye shadow and enough mascara to resurface an asphalt driveway.

With a sigh, Cora braced herself and walked to the bar. A small group of buckle bunnies had converged around the lone cowboy hunched over his beer. The girls were drinking and getting warmed up for a night of debauchery. To his credit, Caleb ignored them as they struggled to get his attention.

Then he looked up and spotted her. He blinked twice, and his face lit up like a kid's at Christmas.

Emboldened by his reaction, Cora lowered her arms, stuck out her chest and walked through the group of girls who eyed her with just enough venom to make her feel a spike of self-satisfaction.

"Waiting for me?" she asked, lowering her voice and looking up at him through her extra-dark lashes.

"All my life," he said, standing up.

Caleb was on fire. He'd taken off his jacket, but his face felt flushed and he was sweating underneath his clothes. The cold beer had done nothing to quench his thirst. Only the knockout brunette standing before him was capable of that—and even then, he doubted he'd ever get enough of her. Ever.

He took her hand and kissed it gently. Before she could roll her eyes at him, he pulled her close and kissed her mouth so tenderly that those beautiful eyes slid closed and she collapsed against him. Her tiny moan of pleasure vibrated against his lips, making his entire body clench like a fist.

Immediately in danger of losing his shit and dragging her into the nearest dark corner to have his way with her, Caleb broke their kiss and looked away. He took out his wallet, dropped a few bills on the bar and put his jacket back on.

"Let's get out of here." His voice had cracked. Embarrassed, he cleared the frog out of his throat, and she smiled at him shyly as though they were on a first date, instead of longtime friends with benefits, instead of lovers, instead of whatever it was they were and whatever he hoped in his heart of hearts they'd become.

Their seats were so close to the action that they could smell the dirt of the arena, heady and earthy with just a tinge of manure. Caleb watched everything through Cora's eyes—the pyrotechnics and flash impressed her, and he liked the way her breath caught during the national anthem when the singer hit the high note and sustained it, clean and true. Together they cheered when Decker's name appeared on the Jumbotron and when Caleb's brother Dean stepped out into the spotlight with the other two bullfighters.

"What do the bullfighters do?" asked Cora.

"Their job's to protect the riders once they bail out or get bucked off."

Cora's eyes widened. "I don't know if I could face down a bull like that."

Caleb smiled. "My brother's always been a little nuts."

When the first rider was up, Andie joined them, taking the empty seat next to him. The men in their section turned to look at him and Caleb felt ten feet tall, a gorgeous woman on either side of him, dressed to the nines.

Andie chatted nervously about the riders, the bulls, the bullfighters, even the barrel man who led the audience in a stirring rendition of "Cotton-Eyed Joe". When a rider smacked his head against the sawed-off horns of one bull, Andie grabbed Caleb's knee and turned her face into his shoulder.

The rider went limp, tangled up in his rope. Fearlessly, Dean tapped the bull's nose to distract it while another bullfighter yanked the rope loose. The rider fell to the dirt, out cold, and the audience went silent. When the bull returned to its pen, a medical team rushed out and revived the rider. He stood up weakly, supported by two assistants, and the arena went wild with applause.

Later, Decker scored an 80-point ride on Blackjack and a breathtaking 89-point ride on Norm's Nightmare, giving him the highest score of the night and a hefty cash prize. "See you two at the after party!" Andie squealed, giving them both quick kisses before rushing back behind the chutes to meet the champ.

Cora seethed.

She knew she had no right to feel jealous of any woman who got near Caleb. But seeing how Andie touched and fussed over him—and how much he seemed to enjoy it—made Cora feel furious at him and ashamed of herself.

As they rode the escalator down to the street, Caleb stood behind her, his hands on her shoulders. He stroked her neck with the sides of his thumbs.

She decided to bite the bullet and ask him flat out. "Tell me something."

"Sure."

"Were you and Andie ever together?"

He dropped his hands. "Wow."

She turned around and looked at him.

He raised his eyebrows at her. "I can't believe you're asking me that."

"Why not? I'm just wondering."

"Women never 'just wonder'."

"Spare me your thoughts on women and answer the question."

"Andie and me? Together?" He stepped off the escalator and shoved his hands in his pockets. "Almost."

Cora let his "almost" answer hang in the air between them as they walked out into the cold night air. They made their way through the tourists, noise and lights of Times Square, but Cora ignored all of it, trying to be cool under the onslaught of her own messy emotions.

"It's embarrassing," he said at last. "I had a little crush on her. Nothing serious. She's the daughter of the foreman at the Hughes place. I asked her out. She stood me up. Later on, I found out she'd gone and run off with Decker. End of story."

"Was this last year? Valentine's Day?"

Caleb's eyes narrowed and he nodded warily. When Cora kept silent, he asked, "What's wrong?"

"Nothing."

"Nothing, my ass."

Cora hated how he made her feel. She hated how her feelings were getting the better of her here, in the middle of her first trip to New York City, in what was supposed to have been an act of reckless spontaneity with the man she liked best in the world, even though she wouldn't allow herself to admit it. Against her will, tears began to gather in her eyes. "How'd you like it...if I...if I said you were just some kind of consolation prize?"

"Sweetheart." Caleb grabbed her shoulders and turned her to face him.

"Aw shit," she said, choking back a sob. "All this mascara's going to start running. What a horror show."

"Shush." He reached into his pocket and pulled out some Kleenex. "Listen to me, girl. Listen good." He dabbed at her eyes and pressed the rest of the tissue into her hand. "Andie's pretty, but she can't hold a candle to you. Only reason I liked her was 'cuz I hadn't met you yet."

Cora shook her head. "And I gave it up in your truck. First night we met."

"Ain't nothin' to be ashamed of. People get together in all kinds of ways, whether they talk about it or not." He touched her cheek. His hand was warm. "I like a woman with brains. You're the smartest person I've ever met, but you have no idea how sexy you are. No fuckin' clue. In fluffy pajamas or a peekaboo dress—doesn't matter. You're sexy as hell. You blow my mind."

Stunned, Cora sniffled. She smiled weakly at Caleb, who pulled her close, wrapping her up in a solid embrace that made her feel tingly and lightheaded. People swirled past them on the sidewalk, but Caleb didn't let her go.

After a long time, she whispered, "Would your brother mind if we ditched the party?"

Caleb smiled. "Now you're talking."

As always, romantic Caleb quickly gave way to raunchy Caleb.

As soon as the elevator doors closed, he corralled her into the corner, pinned her with his big body and unbuttoned her coat. His green eyes on fire, a sexy smirk on his face, he dragged the hard ridge of his cock against her pubic bone, up and down, making her feel his hunger. His hands cupped her jaw as he kissed her hard, his lips crushing hers, smearing her lip gloss.

"Six months I been waiting for a taste of you."

His rough whisper in her ear made her body clench. Kissing her again, he reached down and grabbed her ass. She lifted her leg and hooked it around his hip, leaning back against the wall of the elevator and breaking their kiss. She stared up at him—her lover, her sexual mentor, her fuck buddy—as he slid two fingers into her mouth.

"Make 'em wet, sweetheart," he said.

She did. The pads of his fingers tasted like almond soap and salt. Then he reached down, slid his fingers under the thin lace of her panties and began to caress her burning flesh.

"You think of me when you touch yourself?" he asked.

She nodded, gasping.

"You make yourself come?"

Another nod.

"Still taking them pills?"

"Yeah."

He lifted an eyebrow at her. "You fuckin' anyone else?"

She shook her head. "Only you, Caleb." His fingers pressed deeper and she gasped. Time for the million-dollar question. "How about you, cowboy?"

His warm breath washed over her neck. "Sweetheart, I've been living like a goddamn monk. Last woman I been with is you."

She was silent.

"Don't believe me?" he asked. "Do or don't. It's the truth."

He smiled his deadly handsome smile at her, and her head swam with pleasure. She grabbed his shoulders and shut her eyes. There was a camera in the corner of the elevator. In her mind's eye, she imagined what the video would show: a broad back and a cowboy hat, a woman's bare leg wearing a cowboy boot, and her face contorted in ecstasy. She was already a heartbeat away from falling apart.

The elevator door slid open with a *ding*. Caleb smiled wickedly at her, withdrawing his hand. "Here we are."

Cora floated along the carpeted hall to their room. He slid the keycard in and pushed on the handle. Smiling, he wrapped his arm around her waist and spun her inside, shutting the door behind them.

In the dark, there was only Caleb: his hands, his lips, his tongue, his scent. Without a word, he plucked her from her coat and lowered the top part of her dress. She wasn't used to being without a bra. Her nipples, rubbed all night by the fabric, were sensitive as hell. He gave each one a lick before his hot lips closed over her right nipple. He suckled her hard.

She cried out and arched against him, the pleasure so sharp that it burned. With a grunt, he reached between her legs, rested the heel of his palm on her bone and pressed down. She couldn't believe the possession in his touch, the way he acted like her entire body belonged to him.

She opened her eyes, but in the complete darkness, it made no difference. He slid down her body, dropping kisses on her breasts, her stomach, her belly. Suddenly his hot mouth pressed against the lacy fabric of her panties. He pulled them aside with his teeth and began to finger her molten core.

He groaned. "So. Good."

When she felt the glide of his lips and tongue on her sex, Cora knew they were going down the rabbit hole tonight.

His hot mouth against her pussy, he almost shocked the orgasm out of her, squandering the slow ride she wanted to take on his face. A little annoyed, she slid away, pulled him up and kissed him deeply, tasting herself on his lips.

Her hands found his fly automatically. She undid his belt buckle and the buttons, then dropped to her knees as she pulled off his jeans and boxers. The smell of him, clean and delectable, plugged right into the pleasure center of her brain.

In a second, his shaft was in her fist. When she popped the swollen head of his cock between her lips, the salty-sweet flavor of his precome filled her mouth. She shivered as every lucid thought fled her brain.

"Yes." He put his hand on the back of her head. His cock swelled.

She slid off it, prolonging his pleasure, and flicked the tip of her tongue gently against his balls, feeling the cool weight of them against her lips.

"You...fucking...tease," he murmured, flexing his hips. "I don't even have my boots off yet."

Feeling powerful, she returned her attention to his cock. After licking it like a Popsicle, she circled the base with her thumb and forefinger and slid him slowly into her mouth. Making a tight seal with her lips, she began to glide back and forth, bearing down with her throat muscles and making him collapse against the wall, a big man brought down by the pleasure she gave him.

"I can't," he grunted.

He pulled himself from her mouth, grabbed her arms and yanked her up. Cora gasped as he bent her against the wall, her forearms pressed against the cool plaster.

"Take off them little panties," he growled. "Touch yourself."

She pulled the panties down to where they clung like a sling between her knees. As he rubbed the bare shaft of his cock against her drenched, swollen sex, she reached between her legs and rubbed her slick, hard clit the way he'd shown her. She felt the first twinges of her orgasm threatening to break loose.

"Caleb?" she asked, her voice trembling.

Without warning, he snapped his hips forward and buried his cock deep inside her. Her cry echoed in the empty hotel room and her body screamed at the invasion—months of nothing and, all of a sudden, Caleb's big cock was stretching her open. Delicious pain radiated from her pussy all through her nervous system, vibrating in the tips of her fingers and in the bottoms of her feet.

He pressed deeper, wrapped his arms around her waist and buried his face in her hair. He took a deep breath of her, the inhalation of a drowning man finally breaking the surface.

"Ah Christ Almighty, I missed this. I missed you," he murmured. He reached forward and cupped her breasts with his hands, lightly pinching her hypersensitive nipples and making her inner muscles tighten like a vise around his shaft. She was trembling, overloaded with sensation.

"I missed you too," she whispered.

Months of longing focused to the single point where they were connected and finally whole. She could hear her pussy becoming wetter around him, her body starving for what only he could give her. She bent over and tried to slide off her panties.

With a hiss of annoyance, he grabbed the lacy fabric and ripped them free, dropping them on the floor.

Together, they reached down and rubbed her hard, slick clit with their fingertips. She grunted like an animal, passion washing over her like a monsoon. Her arousal slid in a hot trickle along her inner thighs. He trembled against her. He seemed to be holding back a tidal wave of his own pleasure.

"I'm so close," she hissed.

"It's too much," he gasped. "I can't hold back."

She shut her eyes tight, feeling it all. "Then don't."

At once, Caleb grabbed her breasts and began to ream her, his hard flesh slapping against hers with merciless hunger. A half-dozen strokes and they were both goners.

She exploded just as he did, hard and fast and wild, spinning in a vortex of their own creation, lost in lust, lost in each other.

That first orgasm did nothing to quell Caleb's hunger for her. After they took a quick, wicked shower together, Cora, gloriously naked, turned on the lights and pushed him back onto the bed, her dark eyes darting back and forth between his dick and his face.

He felt himself hardening under the heat of her gaze. His Cora. She'd only slept with him. No other guys had seen her naked or felt the hot pulse of her body the way he had. His cock sprang up and slapped softly against his abs. She took his shaft in her fist and knelt down between his legs.

Still keeping her dark eyes on him, she teased the tip of his cock with the tip of her tongue, then slid her lips over the thick crown. Giving him a preliminary lick, she replaced her mouth with her hand, massaging the tip with the smooth skin of her palm, using his precome to glide over the surface of his skin. Her mouth dipped wickedly lower and she gave his ball sac a long lick before sucking one ball gently into her hot mouth, and then the other. He thought he'd died and gone to heaven.

She released him and whispered, "I missed this."

She stood up straight and straddled his thighs. Automatically, he leaned back and helped her fit his cock into her tight, gorgeous pussy. She sank down and canted her hips forward and backward, moving in a liquid figure eight that took his breath away.

He put his hands on her hipbones and lifted her forward in time with her pivots. The tips of his fingers dug into her supple flesh as she leaned forward and stole a kiss from his lips.

"My sweet Cora," he said.

He sat up slightly and gave each of her nipples a long lick. The rosy tips hardened against his tongue.

"What do you want?" she whispered.

"Ride me, girl."

Smiling, she leaned back and began to bounce against him, her sweet ass cheeks slapping softly against the tops of his thighs. Going deeper, she hissed loudly between her teeth, and a dark lock of her hair fell forward.

His blood on fire, Caleb reached forward and dragged her head down for another kiss.

"Slow down," he whispered against her lips. "Make yourself feel good."

She did as he told her. Eyes closed, she slowed her movements, using his cock as her sex toy. She squeezed him with her inner muscles before gently sliding off. Again she knelt between his legs and began to give his cock long, slow, sweet pulls with her mouth, sucking it like candy.

"Like to suck cock, sweetheart?" he asked. He knew she liked it when he talked dirty to her.

"*Your* cock, Caleb."

She turned around, giving him full view of her perfect ass, her narrow waist and the flare of her hips. In reverse cowgirl, she slipped his cock again into her swollen pussy, put her hands on his knees and began to ride him hard.

He reached forward and grabbed her ass, the flesh so soft and giving that he groaned deep in his chest, and she laughed, proud of what she did to him.

"I know what you want," she said. "Lie back, cowboy."

Carefully, she planted her feet on the edge of the bed, spreading her legs wide. As she lifted her hips, pulling on his cock with her pussy, he began to thrust upward into her. The position was raunchy and one that she liked as much as he did.

He wrapped his hands around her waist and held her steady as he fucked her, her damp hair dangling in his face. He heard her breathing quicken. Her whole body grew hotter against his. They were beginning to sweat;

the radiator *ping*ed and condensation formed on the windows.

Gasping, Cora stood up and climbed back onto the bed beside him. She got on all fours with her knees on the very edge of the mattress. She wiggled her ass in the air and raised an eyebrow at him.

"How about like this?" she asked.

Smiling, he got off the bed and knelt down on the carpet, his face inches from her pussy. Her flesh was pink and swollen, pillowy and glistening and aching for his touch. Gently, he spread her lips apart with his thumbs and buried his tongue in the little keyhole, drinking down her sweet juice and grazing her throbbing clit with the very tip of his middle finger. She tasted of salt and iron and sugar—like life itself. Caleb drank deep.

When she began to whimper, Caleb stood up, took his cock in his hand and slid it into her tight channel. She gasped and arched her body against him. He licked the salt off the back of her neck like an animal.

"Jesus Christ, the taste of you," he whispered.

With one hand on her rib cage and his other hand buried in her hair, he began to pound into her hard, slapping his body against hers. Some women liked it tender and some liked it hard—his Cora liked it every way, just like he did.

After only a minute, she let out a surprised cry and began to fall apart, grabbing the covers as she collapsed forward, muffling her cry against the bed. He could feel her pussy convulsing around him, pulling him deeper as she came.

"Yeah, girl. Let it out," he said.

Without giving her time to rest, he resumed his thrusts, harder this time, and punctuated his efforts with hard spanks as she whimpered and pushed back, the aftershocks of her orgasm making her more uninhibited. Still buried inside her, he pulled her up off the bed until she stood with her back pressed against his chest. He kissed her neck and squeezed her breasts, stroking the wet tips of her nipples and reaching down to stroke her clit until she was gripping him hard, ready to come again.

"Oh my God," she said.

Carefully, he slipped out of her, laid her on her back on the bed and stared at her in front of him, her perfect nipples hard like candies, still slick from his saliva. Her eyes were glassy as she opened her legs wide for him. He stared at her sex, the tiny patch of dark hair, her silken folds and the glossy core that beckoned him with sweet invitation.

"Your turn to come," she whispered.

Possessed with lust, Caleb climbed on top of her and flipped her on her side. Lifting her right leg and straddling her left, he fed his cock into her tight little pussy.

"Ain't gonna be gentle," he growled. "You ready?"

She nodded.

Pressing on her outside thigh, he fucked her harder than he'd ever fucked her before. As he rubbed her clit with his thumb, he thrust deep, again and again, and all of a sudden she began to come again, screaming.

He stopped for a moment, slid out and, unable to resist, took another long drink from her pussy. She was so drenched that when he drew back, he had to wipe his chin with his hand.

"That's three," he said, smiling at her.

"Never had three in a night before," she whispered hoarsely.

"We ain't done yet."

He sank into her so deep his vision blurred at the edges. Fighting for air, Caleb realized that there was suddenly nothing in the whole universe but this woman and what she did to him, the sweetness of her secrets, the way she gave herself completely to him. He rode her until his lungs burned, knocking her head against the mattress as he struggled for words and air.

"That's it," he whispered.

She grabbed fistfuls of the bedsheets to brace herself.

He exploded, hot come shooting from deep inside his body deep into hers. Sex had never felt so good—every cell in his body vibrated with ecstasy. Riding out the last waves of his climax, he leaned back for a moment and wiped the sweat from his forehead with the back of his arm.

"You okay?" he asked softly.

She smiled and nodded, looking up at his face, his chest, his arms.

He withdrew very gently, then slid the head of his still-rigid cock against her clit. Her mouth opened as she let out a gasp of pleasure. Still disoriented from his orgasm, he slid two fingers inside her and began to massage her clit with his other hand, using his own hot come as the lube to glide against her.

When she fell apart again, Caleb stared in wonder. The smooth walls of her pussy bore down on his fingers, crushing them as she came.

As they lay back on the bed, exhausted, she eyed him with a satisfied smile on her face.

"That's four," he said, wrapping his arms around her.

"Night's still young, cowboy," she replied, laughing softly.

They ordered room service—steak and eggs for him, a big Cobb salad for her. After the food arrived and Caleb tipped the server, Cora made him take off the fluffy white bathrobe and they ate their dinner stark naked, giggling and horsing around on the bed.

Still too giddy to sleep, they watched the second half of an old Van Damme movie and chatted—Cora about school and her classmates, Caleb about his nieces and nephews. Cora felt an ache in her chest when Caleb bragged about being their favorite uncle, because what else could he be? He was fun and sweet beneath the cowboy-tough exterior, the kind of uncle that kids would love to be around.

Caleb turned off the TV, drew the blankets around them and embraced her. He kissed her forehead gently.

"I wish we didn't live so far apart," she said.

"Me too, sweetheart."

She ran her hand up and down his washboard abs and rock-hard chest. Her fingers skimmed the cap of muscle on his shoulder, his solid biceps and his thick forearm marked with a tattoo that said *Heartbreaker*. Cora smiled. He could model underwear on one of those billboards outside in Times Square. "I've met a ton of people at Brown, but none that I feel I can really be myself around," she admitted.

"Why not? I love who you are."

She blinked at his words, wishing for the simpler version of that phrase. "You're the only one who knows me. The real me."

He smiled. "Lucky me."

They were quiet for a moment, listening to each other's breathing in the dark. Cora licked her lips and wondered if now would be a good time to bring up the tough stuff. She took a breath and did it.

"My grandma told me about your dad's funeral. How are you doing?"

Caleb reached down and took her hand, threading his big fingers through her little ones. After a long time, he said, "Better. My mom's got it rough. But we're pulling through."

"I thought about you a lot. But I didn't want to bring it up when you called or texted. Not unless you did first."

He kissed her hand. "I know. That's what I needed at the time. You were my escape."

I want to be more than your escape. She closed her eyes and pushed the thought away.

Caleb stayed quiet, and she decided that he didn't want to say anything else on the subject. Instead of feeling shut out, she empathized with him—he wanted to grieve in his own way, on his own time.

"How about another type of escape, then?" she whispered, sliding her hand down between his legs.

"Do you have your ticket?" she asked.

"Yup. What time does your train leave?"

"A couple hours after your plane."

The glass doors of the terminal seemed to inhale and exhale a steady stream of travelers. Caleb put down his duffel bag and pulled her away from the entrance, close enough that she could hear his next words loud and clear.

"Listen. I didn't come out here because I wanted to take you to the rodeo," he said. "I came to ask you something important."

She frowned. "Three days together and you ask me now? Here?"

He blew out a frustrated breath. "Sweetheart, don't bust my balls just now, okay?" His words had no sharp edges, and when he put his hands on her shoulders and pulled her closer, she let him.

"What is it?" she asked. His wind-whipped cheeks had gone pale and his eyes, usually bright with challenge and mischief, were wide with what looked suspiciously like nervousness. She braced herself.

He licked his lips. "I want to be your boyfriend."

The words stood there blinking for a moment, as though he'd just yanked them from their hiding place in the deepest, darkest room of her heart. But she didn't let herself feel any reflexive joy—she swallowed it down and dragged out all of the old arguments she always used on herself.

"I'm nineteen. Now's not the time for a serious boyfriend," she said automatically.

"Bullshit. I've never met a more mature woman in my entire life. And I've never met anyone who knew who she was better than you know yourself." He shook his head and smiled. "I know you. Whenever you want something—whenever you *let yourself* want something—no one can tell you it's the right time or the wrong time to want it. You just do it."

She couldn't disagree with him. "But you're all the way on the other side of the country."

"Don't worry about that just now. What do you say? Do you want to be my girlfriend?"

"What do you mean, 'don't worry'? Women love you," she said feebly. "They fall all over themselves to flirt with you. What chance do I have as your girlfriend?"

He snorted. "I don't encourage them. But you know how many women I've messed with since you? None. I'm not interested. I only want one. You, you frowning, angry little antiflirt." He kissed her nose.

She felt the warmth radiating from his body and her arms ached to embrace him. But even in the face of his confidence, she knew she had no right to say yes to what he wanted. Their plans were so contrary that to agree to be his girlfriend would be irresponsible. And as much of a rogue as Caleb was, she felt protective of his heart, even when it meant she'd have to protect it from herself. So she stepped back and took a deep breath in an attempt to clear her head.

"What kind of future can we have together?" she said. "You're leaving the Hughes place to work on your family's ranch. I'm trying to get as far away from Oleander as I can. There has to be some kind of trade-off for this relationship. I don't want either of us to give up something important in order to be together. That's not a good foundation for anything."

He smiled, and that distracting dimple appeared again in his cheek.

Why couldn't he take this seriously? As she bit back her annoyance, he said something that changed everything as surely as if he'd pulled the magic carpet out from under her feet to show her she could fly.

"Dean's coming back to the ranch after this bull-riding season's over. With him there, Clark and Daniel don't need me around. I was always shit at it anyway. Much better at fixing the equipment and the cars. Which is why I'm going back to school. In September."

She blinked. "What?"

"Yup. You're looking at a college boy. Got my letter last month. Mechanical engineering at the University of Rhode Island. A thirty-minute drive from Brown. An hour and a half by train. I checked." He smiled. "Now it ain't Ivy League, but it's a good program. And when I'm finished, I can look for a job wherever I want." He paused. "Which is to say, wherever you are."

She stared at him, dumbstruck.

"I haven't told the admissions committee yes or no because I wanted to see how you felt first." He took her hands. "When my dad died, I realized something. My parents lived their lives side by side from the time they were eighteen years old, and they were crazy about each other that whole time. Time passes fast. I don't want to waste another moment pretending you ain't the one for me. If you don't feel the same way, sweetheart, I'll back off for good. Let you live your life in peace." His hands were cold and his voice seemed to crack like a teenager's. "But if there's a chance that you feel the same way—and, goddamn it, I'm not gonna pretend it ain't scary putting myself out there like this—let's get something started. You and me. What do you think?"

Since leaving her hometown, Cora had swum in an ocean of words—books, lectures, notes, essays, arguments, presentations. But here, under the hot green-eyed gaze of Caleb MacKinnon, no words seemed necessary.

She reached for him and he reached for her and they kissed until New York City disappeared beneath their feet, melting into the shimmering night sky over Oleander, and Cora felt upside down and right-side up at the same time.

How can a goodbye feel like a hello?

Cora stood at the foot of the escalator leading up to Caleb's gate. As she looked up at him rising away, her heart raced. She'd be with him in California come summertime. In the fall, they'd come back East together. The idea made her so happy she felt like dancing and crying and laughing all at once.

Caleb looked over his shoulder one more time. His eyes latched like hooks on to hers as though he were alone with her in bed instead of in a busy terminal at JFK. When he reached the top, he tipped his cowboy hat and mouthed the words, *I love you.*

"I love you too," she said aloud. It felt as natural as breathing.

With a parting smile, he disappeared into the crowd.

Ball-busting businesswoman meets no-holds-barred cowboy. He's going to need a longer rope.

Please see the next page for a preview of

Cowboy

Resurrection

Fall in love, embrace restlessness.

—PUNJABI PROVERB

MONICA'S FATHER'S voice was calm. "All we're saying is, it can't hurt to meet him, can it?"

"I don't know, Papa. You know I'm leaving in three months."

In the background, her mother's voice rose sharply. "He's studying to be a urologist at Stanford. Did you tell her that? He'll be right in her area when she moves back to Cupertino."

"*Soniye*, please calm down." Monica's father turned back to the phone. "Did you hear her?"

"Yes, I heard. A urologist." Monica withheld her sigh. "I guess you could give him my number. Tell him to call me."

"Okay, good." Her father lowered his voice. "That should satisfy your mother for now."

Monica smiled. "Thanks, Papa. I've got to go."

"See you at dinnertime, *beti*."

Monica ended the call as she exited the pitted highway. Putting her mother's matchmaking obsession out of her mind, she pulled onto the brand-new blacktop parking lot in front of the Silver Spur. It was still April but already the thermometer in the dashboard of her Prius showed 89 degrees. Two big, dusty pickup trucks took up spaces in the lot. She parked next to them and glanced at her watch. Eleven o'clock.

They sure start drinking early in Oleander.

She opened her car door and desert air flooded the air-conditioned interior. When she took off her suit jacket, the hot wind whipped through her sleeveless silk blouse, pulling the sweat from the surface of her skin and messing up the clips that held her long, wild black hair in place. Monica removed the clips, slung her tote bag over her shoulder and took a deep breath.

You're getting them on your side, one by one. Just do what you do best. He's just another cowboy. Nothing different about him at all.

Tension gathered in Monica's shoulders. She could pep talk herself all she wanted, but she knew the truth.

Dean MacKinnon was not just another cowboy.

Her phone buzzed. She pulled it out of her purse and checked the message.

Are you coming? He's here right now with his brother, but I don't know for how long.

She grinned. The bar owner, Tom Shelton, had had her back ever since she proposed her idea to him back in January.

I'm outside, she texted back. She slipped the phone back into her purse. Her high heels were silent over the hot asphalt as she made her way to the door.

The cool interior of the Silver Spur smelled like new paint and lemon wood polish, not a scent Monica equated with old small-town honky-tonks. Tom stood at the register tallying up some tabs while a pretty woman with red hair sat opposite him at the bar, highlighting passages in a big textbook.

Tom looked up when he saw Monica. "Good. You're here." He lifted the counter of the bar and stepped out. He had a gravelly voice and lots of tattoos. "Monica, meet my girlfriend, Wanda. Wanda, honey, this is the mastermind behind Oleander Rodeo Days."

Wanda's eyes lit up as they shook hands. "Oh, man. Tom won't shut up about you. Says you're doing something awesome for the town."

Monica smiled. "Some see it that way. Others..." She trailed off and scanned the room. At one of the corner tables sat two big men in cowboy hats, chatting quietly and watching a baseball game on TV.

"So he hasn't returned your calls?" Tom asked.

"No," Monica said. "Well, not the last five, anyway."

"I'll introduce you. Don't worry, MacKinnons don't bite."

"That's not what I've heard," Wanda said, raising her eyebrows at Tom.

"You hush, troublemaker." Tom gave his girlfriend a crooked grin before he started across the barroom. Ever since he'd taken over, the Spur had flourished. He was one of the rodeo's first sponsors—a godsend.

Tom brought her over to the table. "'Scuse me, fellas."

The brothers turned around, saw her, and on cue, both of them stood up at once.

Oh, my God.

Monica tried not to gasp out loud, but that was the reaction her body had at being confronted with a pair of giant, handsome men. Both were tanned and a little dusty, dressed in jeans, boots and long-sleeve button-down shirts. Clark was the taller brother, but buff and bearded Dean looked even hotter than the photos Monica had seen of him online. She could smell them where she stood and guessed they'd been working all morning. Warm leather, aftershave, dirt, skin, sweat. In a current state of extended celibacy, her body stood up and said howdy.

"Guys, this is Monica Kaur," said Tom. "Her family just took over the Rambling Ranch Inn. She's on the board of directors for the Oleander Rodeo Association.

Monica, meet Clark and Dean. Their family runs MacKinnon Ranch."

The cowboys tipped their hats, but Dean shot an annoyed glance at Tom.

"Nice to meet you both," she said. "Call me Monica."

"Come join us," said Clark. He pulled out a seat for her, and she sat down. "We're watching the D-backs get whupped. You follow baseball?"

"I'm a Giants fan," said Monica. Clark grumbled good-naturedly, took his seat and turned his attention back to the game. They all knew the one she really wanted to talk to was Dean.

Tom cleared some empty beer glasses, gave Monica a conspiratorial wink and left. Monica leaned toward Dean to keep her voice down under the game.

"You're a hard one to get ahold of," she said cheerfully.

He narrowed his bright blue eyes at her and took a sip of beer. His hand on the pint glass was enormous. "We've already had this conversation over the phone. The answer's still no."

"One no and five unreturned phone calls? It'd take a lot more than that to run me off, Mr. MacKinnon."

Clark turned around and waved his hand. "Naw, none of that mister stuff. Call him Dean. Or Uncle Frowny Face. That's what our nieces and nephew call him."

Monica wasn't sure if having Clark's assistance was a good or a bad thing. On one hand, it helped to have an ally. On the other, Dean was looking more annoyed by the second.

"Before you tell me yes or no," she said, reaching into her tote bag, "just let me show you what we have planned." She pulled out her tablet and loaded the website one of her friends from Berkeley had designed for the rodeo association. It was clean, professional and modern. "Here's our home page. And our schedule. Here's where visitors can buy tickets. Take a look."

Monica walked Dean through the website, just as she had for dozens of people before him. Rodeo performances on Friday, Saturday and Sunday. A parade down Main Street. A rodeo dance. The crowning of a rodeo queen.

Dean said nothing, just sat there with his beer in his hand looking blankly at the screen. Clark lost interest in the game and kept his eyes glued on her tablet.

"What do you have lined up for the performances?" Clark asked.

She opened the link. "Bareback riding, barrel racing, ladies' breakaway roping, saddle bronc riding, steer wrestling, tie-down roping, team roping and bull riding, of course." She'd given herself a crash course on all of the events, courtesy of the Internet. "Finals on Sunday, with cash prizes."

"Who's sponsoring?" Clark asked.

"Tom got me Los Angeles Nightlife Group, plus his alcohol distributor and Tioga Beer. We've got the local radio station, the TV station and the *Oleander Oracle*. A dozen local businesses are all doing their part: Johnson Saddlery, the Chevy dealership, a couple of ranches, a couple of farms. It helps that all the proceeds go to the Oleander Fire Department."

"Not all proceeds," said Dean at last. Caught in his icy stare, Monica thought briefly about the videos of him she'd watched online. He regularly stared down 1,800-pound bulls and never flinched.

"What do you mean by that?" she asked, keeping her voice calm and even.

"I mean, Oleander Rodeo Days was your idea, wasn't it? What's your angle?"

"No angle, Mr. MacKinnon. Just bringing business to a town that needs it."

"And a motel that needs more guests, maybe?" He put down his empty glass.

"Who wouldn't mind a little extra business?" She smiled brightly. *Uncle Frowny Face, indeed.*

"It's a half-baked idea," he said flatly. "You've got Oleander Rodeo Days scheduled in a tight window between two major rodeos in the Central Valley. Both are professional shows that draw big crowds. Your local competitors are going to save up their time and money for one or the other, not for some amateur show in some Podunk town."

Before Monica could respond, Clark piped up. "Jeez, lighten up, Dean."

"Just callin' it as I see it." He shrugged and leveled his eyes on her.

Monica pressed her lips together. Why did that gaze have to be so direct? Up close his eyes were an extraordinary shade of blue, like swimming pools in the desert. Dean's arm was pressed against hers. She felt his hot, hard biceps through the thin cotton of his shirt. Suddenly she wondered what it would be like to run her hands over his bare arms, to touch his muscles and all those scars she knew he was hiding under his clothes.

She blinked and concentrated on the conversation at hand. "Everything you're saying is true," she said, "which is why I need you." She powered down her tablet. "Make an appearance at this event. Let us put your name on the marquee. It'd be a really wonderful draw for attendees. You're a local legend."

A crease formed between his eyebrows and he looked disgusted, as if he'd just stepped in a fresh cow patty. Monica quickly realized such a trivial thing as bullshit wouldn't bother a man like him, but the expression on his face told her he was about to turn her down.

She spoke before he could. "Before you tell me yes or no," she said again, "I'd like to show you the arena and get your take on it. As someone who's seen hundreds of rodeo venues. Please. You're an expert. I'd like to know your thoughts."

"You know, this is just a lunch break for us," he said. "We're heading back—"

"Go with her, Dean," said Clark. "I'm gonna watch a few more innings anyway."

Dean said, "But—"

"We'll catch up this afternoon," said Clark, waving his hand. "You two take your time."

Still not allowing Dean to say a word, Monica stood up. "And the inn is not far from here."

Clark watched his brother with an expectant face. Outnumbered, Dean grimaced one more time, pushed his chair back and stood up. "Fine," he said to her. "But you're driving, princess."

It was her turn to grimace. "Right this way, Mr. MacKinnon."

This cowboy and cowgirl sell the steak and the sizzle.

Please see the next page for a preview of

Cowboy Player

I wonder how many people I've looked at all my life
and never seen.

—JOHN STEINBECK

With a grimace, Melody swallowed down the last of her gin and tonic. One of the bartenders whisked her glass away and asked if she wanted another. Even though she did, Melody shook her head.

Something touched her bare arm. A warm fingertip grazed her skin from elbow to wrist. She looked up.

"Lost in thought again?" Clark leaned close and kissed her cheek, just as he had hundreds of times before. One of the Silver Spur's waitresses put a beer down in front of him and flashed a sexy grin. He smiled at the woman briefly and turned his attention back to Melody.

She shook her head. "It must be hard to be you."

"Why do you say that?"

"Women. The endless parade of women fighting for your attention."

"Oh, it's not so bad." Clark took a sip of beer.

"Where are all your brothers? They usually help carry the burden."

"I'm on my own tonight," he said. "But let's talk about you, not me. Why so blue, Mel? Baby sister all grown up?"

They turned to look at the crowd in front of the stage. Harmony had found herself a cowboy admirer. The lucky fellow was holding her close and nuzzling her neck as he led her around the dance floor.

Was Melody sad that Harmony was growing up? No, not exactly. Nostalgic, more like—for a version of herself she wasn't sure ever existed. Had she ever been that young and optimistic? Had she ever let herself be that free?

"I'm proud of her," Melody said at last. "It's been hard. Seeing our mom get sick like that. Lots of kids would've dropped out. But she finished school with a 3.8. This is her first night out in a long, long time."

"A smarty-pants, just like you."

"Smarter than me," said Melody. "She learned something useful. Solid paycheck, helping others, all that good stuff."

"You're a brilliant teacher, from what I've heard."

"Diagramming sentences isn't exactly going to save us from the zombie apocalypse, now is it?"

"If there's a zombie apocalypse, nothing will save us, Mel. The only thing left to do is get drunk and screw." He held up his beer mug and winked at her. An honest-to-goodness wink.

Melody shook her head. "You can't help yourself, can you, MacKinnon? You're a hopeless flirt."

"Flirting? Thought I was just drinking beer and being myself." He looked down at the empty coaster in front of her. "What about you? What are you having? Gin and tonic, right?"

He remembered her favorite drink. Melody smiled. "No, I'm good. I'm on sister watch tonight. She really wants to cut loose. Someone's gotta hold her hair back when the vomit flies. Which it inevitably will." She waved her hand at him. "You should go have a good time. Get yourself a nice piece. Enjoy your Saturday night."

Only Clark could make a shrug look so sexy. "But I'm already enjoying my Saturday night."

Something about the way he said those words made Melody's skin tingle.

As an experiment, she uncrossed her legs and leaned forward, resting her arms on the bar. For a nanosecond, Clark's dark eyes darted to her cleavage before resting on his beer. A sudden, electric thrill shimmied down her spine. Her body clenched with pleasure, knowing she could still get the attention of a man as insanely hot as Clark MacKinnon.

But then...guilt.

That's Clark. Don't flirt with Clark.

The band started playing something loud and rowdy. Clark leaned forward. As he spoke into her ear, his warm breath caressed the sensitive skin on her neck. "You know, Lucky's going to be doing the rodeo circuit soon. It'll be just you and me on the road. Hours and hours together. You ready for that, Mel?"

Melody cleared her throat. *Be cool. Make a joke. Keep your distance.* "You and me and a couple hundred pounds of raw meat? Sounds kinky, Superman."

In the crowded bar, Clark stood flush against her, his arm pressed against hers. The sleeves of his dark T-shirt molded to the broad muscles in his biceps. Where the cotton ended, his skin was smooth and hot. She'd spent enough time with Clark shut up in the van to know he smelled pretty good—soap and leather, a little drugstore aftershave. Up close was a different story. That familiar smell, mixed with the subtle scent of his skin, made the transmission fall out of Melody's self-control.

"I had a feeling you might be kinky, Santos," he said.

He moved even closer. With gentle fingers, he brushed her long hair away from her neck and tucked the curls behind her ear. Intentionally or not, his bottom lip brushed her earlobe as he whispered, "Am I right?"

Christ. Heat rushed like quicksilver to her core, leaving her fingers and toes tingling with cold. She hadn't been this turned on in months, maybe years. Under the bar, she pressed her thighs together to ease the hot ache that Clark had summoned with nothing more than a few whispered words and the caress of his fingertips.

"Clark, what are you..." She trailed off and looked into his eyes.

Was he teasing her? Was he serious?

She and Clark had played in the creek together as little kids and slammed each other with dodgeballs in the schoolyard. She'd spent years in his company and yet, she couldn't remember what color his eyes were. Here in the neon light, she couldn't see his irises. But she could feel the unfamiliar heat of his gaze burning her like a thousand suns. Coming from a friend or lover, that look meant desire. That look meant sex.

The band finished the song with a loud holler and a wild drum solo. The crowd cheered. Clark locked his eyes on her for a half-second more before Tom Shelton, the big, tough-looking bartender, set down a row of shot glasses on the bar in front of them.

"Hey, Clark. Hey, Mel." Tom proceeded to fill the shot glasses from a bottle of cinnamon-scented whiskey.

Clark blinked and looked up at Tom. Melody folded her hands and rested them on her knees to keep from trembling.

"Your brothers here tonight?" Tom asked Clark.

Clark cleared his throat and shook his head. "No. All of 'em are busy."

"That's a first. How about you? What are you two up to?"

"Just keeping an eye on Mel's little sister."

"No kidding. She's a live wire," said Tom. "These shots are for her group, matter of fact."

Melody leaned back and glanced at the bar where Harmony's friends were sitting, but her little sister wasn't there. Melody looked back at the dance floor. Harmony and her new cowboy friend were nowhere to be seen.

"Clark." She hopped off the barstool. "I've lost sight of my sister. Can you see her?"

A full foot taller than Melody, Clark stood up straight and scanned the crowded room. "She was right there a minute ago."

"Ah, Christ," Melody said.

"We'll find her. She can't have gotten far." Clark grasped Melody's hand in his. With a warm, steady grip, he led her through the crowd, cutting a path for her. Together, they searched the dance floor and the area by the pool tables. They walked down the hallway leading to the restrooms and the smoking patio—still no Harmony. They were almost to the parking lot when Melody saw a flash of glitter in the corner of her eye.

In the darkest corner of the bar, tucked into a booth, Melody's baby sister was straddling a cowboy and sucking his face off like a lamprey on a dead flounder. The cowboy's big hands gripped the backs of Harmony's bare thighs and together they looked like they were doing a very private dance in public.

"What the hell!" Melody exclaimed. "Harmony!"

Harmony popped up, surprised. Her lipstick was smeared across her mouth and one strap of her dress hung off her shoulder. "Holy shit, Mel!" she exclaimed. She looked between Melody and Clark and after a couple of seconds, began to giggle. She was drunk as a skunk. "You two look like you've seen a ghost."

"Yeah, the ghost of my sister's dignity." Melody went over and adjusted Harmony's dress. "Get up. We're going home."

"What? Why?"

"Why? Because drinking is fine. Dancing is fine. Having sex in public? Not fine." Melody grabbed Harmony's wrist and pulled her to her feet.

"Easy now," Clark said softly. He took Harmony's elbow and helped her get her balance.

Melody looked into the dark booth to see who'd taken advantage of her sister. "You've got some nerve. She's wasted. I have a mind to call the cops on you."

The guy held up his hands. "Please don't call the cops." His words were slurred. He was as drunk as Harmony. "I just did what Clark said to do and the next thing I know—"

Melody knocked the hat off the cowboy's head to get a look at his face. "Holy fuck! Lucky!"

He blinked. "I'm so sorry, Melody. We just got carried away."

Behind her, Clark let out a hoot. When Melody glared at him, he pressed his lips together, but his eyes were still laughing. "No harm done, Mel," he said, holding Harmony up as she swayed on her feet. "Come on. Let's get these two train wrecks home."

ALSO BY MIA HOPKINS

The Cowboy Cocktail Series
Cowboy Valentine
Cowboy Resurrection
Cowboy Player
Cowboy Karma
Cowboy Rising

The Kings of California Series
Deep Down
Hollywood Honkytonk

ABOUT THE AUTHOR

Mia Hopkins writes lush romances starring fun, sexy characters who love to get down and dirty. She's a sucker for working class heroes, brainy heroines and wisecracking best friends. She lives in Los Angeles with her roguish husband and waggish dog.

For more information, please visit her website at www.miahopkinsauthor.com.